DEATHLESS DAN
KNOCKED ON HIS CAN!

Longarm had just been fixing to yell, "Freeze!"
when the proddy cuss in the raccoon coat broke stride
to drop into a gunfighter's crouch and fire both Schofields in turn. So Longarm let fly with both barrels
of his sawed-off shotgun at once, just in case he'd
been killed.

He hadn't been.

They'd later find two bullet holes that had closely
bracketed his broad shoulders in the plank fence behind him. His double charge of number-nine buck
blew his own target a good two paces back along that
flagstone walk to land flat with a smoking six-gun
out to either side in the frost-covered grass.

"You're the one they call Longarm," the man at
his feet declared in a sort of dreamy way, softly adding, "I'm going to get you, too, as soon as I feel a
mite better."

— TABOR EVANS —

LONGARM

AND THE SADDLE ROCK SPOOK

J

JOVE BOOKS, NEW YORK

LONGARM AND THE SADDLE ROCK SPOOK

A Jove Book / published by arrangement with the author

PRINTING HISTORY
Jove edition / November 1995

ISBN: 0-515-11746-3

A JOVE BOOK®
Jove Books are published by The Berkley Publishing Group,
200 Madison Avenue, New York, New York 10016.
JOVE and the "J" design are trademarks
belonging to Jove Publications, Inc.

PRINTED IN THE UNITED STATES OF AMERICA

10 9 8 7 6 5 4 3 2 1

LONGARM

AND THE
SADDLE ROCK SPOOK

Chapter 1

The frost was on the pumpkin, and most everything else along the Front Range that dark October dawn, as Deputy U.S. Marshal Custis Long of the Denver District Court resisted the temptation to stamp his freezing feet in a cinder-paved alley behind the house of ill repute. He hadn't been sent up to the Wyoming line just to serenade whores with his boot heels. The town law up here in Saddle Rock had wired a tip on a federal want they weren't about to take on without a whole lot of help.

Deathless Dan Marlow was reputed to be insane. He was a killer for certain. They called him Deathless Dan because he'd been shot up a dozen times or more and refused to die. The fourteen men Marlow had shot hadn't managed that trick, and three of the eight lawmen on the rascal's list had been federal.

So Longarm, as he was better known to friend and foe alike, stood shivering in that alley by the dawn's early light with a ten-gauge, double-barreled and sawed-off Greener in his gloved hands, and with his federal badge pinned to the breast of a sheepskin jacket that wasn't half thick enough. He didn't know Marlow on sight, and many a less guilty old boy might have cause to tear out the back door of a whorehouse when a pack of lawmen proceeded to pound in from out front.

In the meantime, what in thunder was keeping that from happening? The ruse depended on a wanted man's natural inclination to choose the way out that seemed less risky. A dash through tricky light to what might seem an empty alley had to have a stand-up fight in a lamplit hallway beat. But the choice was sure to get less obvious as it got ever brighter outside.

Longarm had posted himself in a shallow slot formed by one corner of a carriage house and a board fence facing the back gate and crap-house of Madame Laverne's establishment. The whores who'd turned in Deathless Dan as a man who'd overstayed his welcome said he never crossed the yard to use that crapper, but always had the gals fetch and carry chamber pots to the room he'd chosen. That sounded like an easy way to wear out an old boy's welcome. A flagstone walk from the back door of the three-story whorehouse to the open gateway, facing the alley, pointed like an arrow at Longarm's poor cover. It was getting poorer by the moment as the sun rose ever higher in that autumn overcast.

Longarm was fixing to move across the alley to huddle against the back of the whorehouse crapper when the back door popped open to spill lamplight and a whore in a silk kimono out on the back steps.

Whether the gal was in on the sellout or not, she went through all the right motions. If she saw Longarm across the alley as she peered all about with her breath steaming in the morning chill, she never let on. She ducked back inside and, sure enough, a taller figure came out the door wearing a peaked winter cap with ear flaps and a racoon calf-length coat Longarm sort of envied. The son of a bitch was gripping a Schofield .45 in each bare hand. So Longarm just waited as the fur-coated stranger came down that walk as far as the back gate.

Then it got sort of noisy.

Longarm had just been fixing to yell "Freeze!" when the proddy cuss in the racoon coat broke stride to drop into a

2

gunfighter's crouch and fire both Schofields in turn. So Long-arm let fly with both barrels of his sawed-off shotgun at once, just in case he'd been killed.

He hadn't been. They'd later find two bullet holes that had closely bracketed his broad shoulders in the plank fence behind him. His double charge of number-nine buck blew his own target a good two paces back along that flagstone walk to land flat with a smoking six-gun out to either side in the frost-covered grass.

Longarm set the spent shotgun atop an alley trashcan, and reached in under his sheepskins for his own .44-40 double-action Colt before he got any closer to Deathless Dan, if that was who he'd just killed. A lawman could kill the wrong man and just say he was sorry in one of Ned Buntline's dime magazines. But in real life they surely made you fill out a heap of tedious papers.

As he moved in he saw twin streams of blood flowing along the walk like steaming lava. Steam was rising from the pile of bloody fur as well. None of that was as surprising as the fact that the son of a bitch suddenly declared, in an oddly conversational tone, "I'm going to get Madame Laverne for this. I know it was her who betrayed me for the price upon my head."

Longarm kept the astoundingly tough rascal covered as he told him not unkindly, "You got some healing and hanging to get through first. I'd be Deputy Custis Long, and I sure hope I have the honor of addressing the one and original Deathless Dan Marlow from York State by way of Fort Reno, from which you deserted in time of war. I'd like to know because, no offense, there's heaps of medium-sized and middle-aged gents with eyebrows that meet in the middle."

"You're the one they call Longarm," the man at his feet declared in a sort of dreamy way. "I'm going to get you too, as soon as I feel a mite better."

Then someone else called out from the house, "Is that you

3

in that sheepskin jacket, Deputy Long? I could swear I heard him blazing away with them Schofields first!''

Longarm called back modestly, ''He did. He missed me. I ain't the one claiming immortality back here. I'll be whipped with snakes if I can see why this rascal is still alive. But he seems to be. So we ought to get him a doctor.''

Then, as the town constable, a kid deputy, and Smiley and Dutch, federal deputies, from the Denver office, came along the walk to join him, Longarm dropped to one knee to gingerly open the front of that steaming raccoon coat with his free hand.

Then he whistled softly down at what seemed a plate of raspberry jam stuck to a tattered wool vest and called out, ''Forget what you just heard me say about a sawbones. He wasn't so deathless after all.''

Then the man he'd downed with an awesome double ten-gauge blast took another breath and weakly murmured, ''Nobody can kill me. I am the one having this dream. If I was to die, or just wake up, the whole bunch of you would be gone like soap bubbles, see?''

Then he coughed up a big spongy lump of bloody lung tissue, and the next time Longarm felt the side of his neck there was no pulse to be felt. The town law, an older gent called Crabtree, hunkered down at Longarm's side and quietly observed, ''He must have been wrong. We still seem to be here.''

Longarm grimaced and replied, ''I have a better grasp on what was ailing him now. Them alienist docs who study criminal minds say heaps of them are stuck in childhood, where they feel like they're the only ones who really matter. This son of a bitch wasn't half as brave as your average honest working-man. He thought nobody could ever kill him, and it didn't matter how many others *he* might kill, because this whole world around him was one big playroom he'd whipped up for his own enjoyment!''

''Well, they said he was a homicidal lunatic,'' Constable

4

Crabtree observed in a laconic tone.

Longarm replied, "I just said that. Such odd notions can be catching. So before we plant this immortal rascal in the cold, cold ground, I'd as soon have some photographs taken of him. Didn't I see a photographer's studio near the depot as we were getting off the train last night?"

Crabtree's young deputy, Nat Hayward, volunteered, "They won't open before nine. But I know where the artistical gals live. You want me to go fetch 'em?"

Longarm started to nod. Then he decided, "Ain't no big emergency. I doubt this meat will spoil before regular business hours in this fall weather. You say that photograph place is infested with *gals*?"

"French gals," Nat Hayward replied. "They ain't *wicked* French such as the one Madame Laverne has on tap inside. The Madamy-Zills Demille learned photography in France, where some Frog called Dagger up and invented the whole notion."

Longarm was too polite to correct the well-meaning kid. He wasn't dead certain how you pronounced Daguerre in any case.

By this time Smiley and Dutch had hunkered down on the far side of the steaming pile of shotgunned meat. Smiley was the poker-faced deputy's family name. Nobody could pronounce the real name of the one they called Dutch. Smiley was the more thoughtful of the pair. So it was he who quietly asked, "Why do you want them French gals to take pictures of this ugly pile of shit, pard?"

Longarm replied, "In case anyone ever accused me of putting the wrong pile of shit on the ground. I know he answers to the descriptions we had on Deathless Dan. I know he just now told me he thought he was deathless. But I still want photographs taken of his hooked nose and funny eyebrows before they nail his coffin shut over 'em. It's a real pain in the ass when some penny-dreadful writer decides the real Vasquez or Black Jack Slade is still out there stopping stagecoaches be-

5

cause none of us dumb lawmen knew who we were hanging, or worse yet, because we took a bribe to hang some innocent cuss.''

Constable Crabtree nodded soberly and said, ''I follow your drift. The folks offering bounty money on this owlhoot rider will want more than just our word before they part company with it too.''

So later that same morning, as what was left of Deathless Dan lay at a handy angle on a cellar door, the not-too-young but not-so-bad-looking Demille sisters, Paulette and Marie, took close-up pictures, from more than one angle, of the late immortal killer. They'd bill the Justice Department more than your average cowhand had to pay for his own fool portrait framed and on sepia-tone paper.

Nobody cared. Everyone who'd ever seen the real Deathless Dan in life agreed that had to be him in death as soon as they were shown a print of that blankly staring cadaver. So that seemed to be that, and the waters of more than one spring thaw flowed under the bridges as Longarm brought many another bad man to justice and quite a few bad girls to bed.

He'd almost forgotten that brief encounter with Deathless Dan Marlow when he arrived at work a tad late, one balmy September morning in Denver, to be told by young Henry, the clerk who played the typewriter out front, that their boss, Marshal William Vail, was anxious to see him and not in a very good mood at all.

So Longarm lit a three-for-a-nickel cheroot in self-defense as he ambled toward Billy Vail's inner office to see what he'd done this time.

His conscience was clear. He hadn't been in any fights at either the Black Cat or Parthenon Saloon. The only two gals he'd slept with that week were neither married up nor spoken for, and he was wearing the infernal shirt and tie the Hayes Administration demanded under a store-bought tobacco-tweed

6

suit that wouldn't need cleaning or pressing before payday.

He took a deep drag on his own cheap tobacco and entered the blue haze filling Billy Vail's oak-paneled office as if it lay somewhere off the Grand Banks of Nova Scotia. But instead of a foghorn he heard Billy's voice ominously declaring, "I have been under the impression for going on three years that you and the other deputies I sent up to Saddle Rock after Deathless Dan Marlow had seen them *bury* the murderous son of a bitch!"

Longarm groped his way to the one leather chair on his side of the cluttered desk as he calmly replied, "As a matter of fact the lady who turned him in for a cut of the reward paid for a handsome funeral and let them plant him in a sandstone mausoleum she'd bought for a couple of her whores in the Signal Rise Cemetery. Some of the more refined folks in Saddle Rock seemed a mite offended. I figured she made the gesture lest some of Marlow's pals suspect she hadn't been as fond of him. Lord knows she could afford it, considering all that bounty you wouldn't let Smiley, Dutch, or me put in for."

The older, shorter, and fatter lawman on the far side of the fog bank rumbled, "Never you mind my policy on blood money. I just now went over your old report and had Henry dig them sepia prints out of the files for me. Now I want you to scamper down to the Union Station and see if you can still make the afternoon Burlington to Cheyenne. If you can I want you to get up to Saddle Rock with them old pictures and compare 'em with some newer ones. The first was taken independently by a schoolmarm with her own box camera. The second was taken by a professional, shooting inside a whore house you may remember, for an Eastern magazine story about us Wild Western folk. Saddle Rock is sending us extra prints. But they ain't here yet and I figure you can get on up and wire me yes or no this evening. See what you think, and send the wire by day rates to my home address on Capitol Hill no matter *what* you think.''

To which Longarm could only reply, ''Wait a minute. What are you asking me to compare with our pictures of a long-gone outlaw, Boss?''

Vail snorted another octopus cloud of pungent smoke and told him in no uncertain terms, ''Pictures of the same son of a bitch alive and well, of course. Before you blather about old photographs, that schoolmarm wasn't working in Saddle Rock the day you watched 'em put Marlow away, or so you thought. They've since built a frame schoolhouse and hired her to run it. She was so proud that this very June she lined up all her students, and took their picture out front. A gent standing off to one side ain't looking at the camera, and may not have known just what she was up to as she snapped him as well. It was the professional who developed her plate later who noticed she'd shot a full-length portrait of Deathless Dan Marlow, or his identical twin.''

Longarm thought back before he declared, ''Marlow had no siblings of any description. I went over his past in some detail before I handed in my report. Must have just been some jasper who looked something like the dead man. Might not look at all the same if he was photographed at another angle.''

Vail shook his bullet head and growled, ''It seems he does. He next appears as one of the crowd in Madame Laverne's plush taproom, *that* photograph taken by another person with another camera. But now let's get to the spooky parts. The photography lab naturally showed the odd pictures to Constable Crabtree, who was there when you shotgunned what was supposed to be Deathless Dan. So Crabtree naturally showed prints of the pictures around town. Guess how it goes from there.''

Longarm shrugged. ''Nobody in a small trail town could say who the strange face belonged to? That's no great mystery, Billy. The town lies betwixt a railroad spur line and that old

8

Goodnight cattle trail. Most any number of gents, looking like most anyone, could have just been passing through.''

Vail said, ''You're going to miss that train.''

So Longarm rose to his feet and reached across the desk for the envelope of old photographs, even as he complained, ''I'm on my fool way, but I wish I knew why. Even if this mysterious stranger turns out a dead ringer for Deathless Dan Marlow, and even if I can catch up with him, what am I supposed to do about it?''

''Arrest him,'' said Billy Vail flatly.

Longarm smiled down uncertainly as he put the envelope away in a side pocket of his frock coat. ''On what charge? Just being sort of homely? I know a gent over on Tremont Place who looks like that Bill Chadwell who used to ride with the James-Younger gang. But I'd sure look dumb arresting a barber who looks like a dead bandit. Bill Chadwell was killed back in '76 and—''

''Constable Crabtree was killed on a Saturday night, in front of a dozen witnesses,'' Vail declared, ''He'd caught up with this dead ringer for Deathless Dan near the railroad stop. He demanded to know why the beetle-browed and hook-nosed cuss had just run Madame Laverne out of town with all her gals and municipal taxes. The man who looks just like Deathless Dan Marlow acted just like Marlow was inclined to at such times. He drew two guns and fired both of them point-blank at Constable Crabtree. Then he sweetly asked if anyone in sight felt like dancing with him, and when nobody did, he simply walked away in the gathering dusk. Some say he seemed to be headed for that graveyard you mentioned. But you know how some witnesses are.''

Longarm grimaced and declared, ''I'll find out exactly which way he went. I sort of liked old Constable Crabtree.''

Chapter 2

It hardly seemed worth it until you studied on it. But seeing
he'd had the time to prepare and you just never knew, Longarm
got aboard that northbound Burlington with his McClellan saddle and possibles, a Winchester '73 keeping company with his
bedroll and packed saddlebags. He figured it was safer to drag
them along and never need them than need them and not have
them when what seemed a simple chore got a tad complicated.

Seeing his train ride would only last a few hours, counting
a change to that spur line at Fort Collins, Longarm decided
he'd best pass on the delights of the club car and just tough it
out in a day coach, with his saddle and such sitting beside him.
The mid-afternoon train left Denver half empty, seeing most
honest folks were still at work on a weekday. Anyway, Longarm usually preferred to ride alone.

He reconsidered the way he discouraged company when a
well-proportioned brunette in summer-weight widow's weeds
and a perky veiled hat got on with her own carpetbag as the
train was fixing to leave.

She looked sort of familiar, and he'd found widow women
tended to either cut a man dead or get familiar as all get-out
on short notice.

But he saw she'd already chosen her own lonesome seat, with that carpetbag perched beside her. And what the hell, he'd be getting off before he'd had time for anything like a smooth approach. So he forced himself to lean back, light a cheroot, and haul out the papers from his office. There hadn't been time to pick up a good magazine back in Denver and the scenery outside was tedious until you got out on the High Plains aprons of the Rockies, north of the Denver yards.

He opened the plain envelope Billy Vail had handed across the desk to him. He hadn't examined the half-dozen sepia-tones of that cadaver posing on a cellar door for a spell. But old Deathless Dan looked as dead as ever. By the time they'd gotten him across town and posed in that bitter cold, his big nose had taken on that sharp waxy look you only saw in the dead or dying. Those half-opened eyes also looked lively as raw oysters on chopped ice. Anyone that ugly, who'd been seen around Saddle Rock of late had to be somebody else entirely.

That seemed much more possible than Deathless Dan busting out of that sandstone mausoleum to have fresh photographs taken. Longarm idly wondered whether those recent prints would turn out to be black and white or this sort of murky sepia-tone. He'd forgotten the mild argument about that he'd had with Miss Paulette, the older and bossier Demille sister, way back when.

The most up-to-date photography involved printing a positive image on special paper from a glass-plate negative. Then the developer printed the final results in plain old black and white, the cheap way, or in that more artistic and, some said, more realistic-looking sepia-tone, with shades of brown from almost black to a creamy white.

Longarm had to admit the sun-tanned flesh tones and straw-colored hair of blondes came out more natural in a sort of autumn haze when you printed a sepia-tone photograph. But some of the detail often seemed fuzzy. That was why Longarm

11

had asked the Demilles to supply him with sharp-focus black and white prints. But talking sense to artistic gals was a chore, even when they spoke better English.

Longarm put the old sepia-tones back in the envelope, put that in his coat pocket again, and read over the onionskins young Henry had typed up both three years ago and more recently.

One was a copy of his own report on the track-down and shootout. Longarm read it over again, just in case he hadn't been remembering things right.

He saw his memory was sharp enough. It hadn't been a Viking saga that went on and on like that song about the gal with the ring-dang-do. He put his report away with the photographs, ran over the dead man's nasty if somewhat tedious criminal history again, and said aloud, "You told us how you felt this old world was your personal doll house, and how you liked to bite the heads of the dollies packing badges. So I'll allow a mean kid like you would gun a nice old constable if you'd be kind enough to tell me how in blue blazes even you could manage that. I put two ten-gauge charges of number-nine buck in you, old son. Then I got a second opinion from the deputy coroner, Doc Kruger. He opened you up from pubis to both nipples, and opined you had fatal doses of lead in your vitals from liver to lights, with your heart nicked seriously. When I mentioned you bragging you were immortal as you lay there, the doc said you must have been tough as hell or mad as a hatter. He said a man might last a few moments with his heart pumping the wrong way or not at all. But he seemed surprised the experience had left you so conversational. He certified you dead for certain as they sewed you back up with butcher's twine. Then they drained all your blood and pumped you full of embalming fluid that makes your eyes water just to sniff at. So no offense, Deathless Dan, you were one dead son of a bitch when they nailed you in that box and tucked you away with them dead whores behind a locked bronze door.''

He put away everything but a copy of the night letter Billy Vail had gotten from a mighty worried Saddle Rock town council. It seemed they'd left Constable Crabtree's senior deputy, Nat Hayward, in charge of law and order around the town, pending the coming fall elections. Longarm knew he might be remembering a kid deputy unfairly. It had been a few years since the big stupid-looking kid had been getting in his way up yonder. Lawmen got wiser as they got older, or they didn't get older. Nat Hayward was likely old enough to shave regular now.

Lord, how the years of a man's life slipped through his fingers like grains of sand, and wasn't it something how that neighborhood kid who'd been playing jacks out front when Longarm had first moved into his furnished digs in Denver was pushing a damned baby buggy nowadays.

Longarm read over the terse words from Saddle Rock a good three times as the train carried him ever closer to the scene of all that mysterious bullshit. He got out his own notebook and wrote down the names of some witnesses. He'd worry about the few loose ends in the night letter when he had somebody in front of him to question. All he really had to go on at the moment, if half of it was true, was that someone who looked a lot like Deathless Dan Marlow had come back to Saddle Rock, or maybe come to Saddle Rock for the first time, to run a whore out of town, to gun the town law, and to make some others mighty nervous.

Longarm put everything away and admired the scenery outside for a million years as he smoked at least a hundred pounds of tobacco. And then they were slowing down for Fort Collins and he was fighting the impulse to get up and grab his Mc-Clellan before he had to. Longarm liked to think of himself as an experienced traveler, and some obvious cowboys and Indians were already crowding the front end of the car with a good two miles to roll.

That handsome widow woman wasn't acting excited either. She just sat there with one dainty hand resting on the hand grips of her carpetbag. He wondered what she'd say if her offered to help her. He decided to quit while he was ahead. His own load would be heavy enough, and for all he knew she was staying aboard to ride on to Cheyenne. Gals could sure look amused when a gent offered help they hadn't asked for and might not need.

As the train slowed to a crawl he rose and, sure enough, she just went on sitting there. So he got down his own load, braced it atop a shoulder with his gun hand free, and mosied forward to make it out to the platform steps as those early birds were dropping off. Longarm had just started down the steel steps when he heard an anguished scream and a soft perfumed form crashed into him. It would have caused a serious accident if Longarm hadn't let go of his saddle to grab a handrail and that yelling widow woman at the same time.

The two of them still wound up in a horizontal position at the bottom of the steps, with her on top and the old army saddle cradling Longarm's skull. Only the Good Lord knew where his hat had gone to.

He grinned up at the face within handy kissing distance and asked if she was all right. She gasped, "No! That man in the checked shirt has my bag! He snatched it from my very hand as he shoved me against you!"

Longarm craned his neck to spot a checked shirt one hell of a ways down the platform and moving fast. So he gently but firmly rolled the far from feathery widow woman off him, and came to his hands and knees as he snapped, "Stay here and keep an eye on *my* stuff! I'm the law and I run pretty good, ma'am."

Then he was up and running, but it wasn't easy. There were

14

others of every description along the cement platform between him and the red brick railroad depot at the far end. The bag snatcher in that foolish shirt crashed into a fat lady just outside the depot waiting room. She hit him with her handbag, which seemed only just, and he dropped the carpetbag he'd snatched, which seemed even better.

Longarm reached down to grab the widow woman's bag without stopping as that fat lady took a swing at *him* with her handbag as well. When he got inside the far darker waiting room it took him a moment to get his eyes working. Once he could see better, there was no checked shirt to be seen. But a lot of the folks seated on the hardwood benches seemed to find *him* mighty interesting indeed. So he took a bow and announced, "I am the law and I just now chased a bag snatcher in a checked shirt in here."

Nobody answered. He hadn't expected much more. He sighed and announced, "Like the Chinese philospher said, may you all be cursed with long lives in turbulent times."

Then he headed back the other way, hoping he was wrong about another thought he'd just had. He didn't spot that gal in widow's weeds right off, and started muttering, "Damn it, your dear old mother warned you about strange women throwing themselves in your arms!"

Then he saw her, by his McClellan and possibles, further up the platform than he remembered. He still checked his wallet as he strode to rejoin her, calling out, "He gave me the slip, but ain't this your bag he dropped along the way, ma'am?"

She clapped her hands like a schoolgal and declared him a saint on the spot. He told her to hold the thought until she'd made sure all her valuables were still there. So she hunkered down in her long black skirts to do so, murmuring even more nice things about him as she pawed through her unmentionables. Longarm was too polite to watch too closely. He had his wallet, watch, derringer, and such. There was hardly any decent

15

way a gent could ask a lady to shift her ass and let him go through saddlebags he'd asked her to watch for him. He thought hard, and decided there was nothing worth insulting a lady for in either saddlebag. He could see she hadn't lifted his Winchester, and what the hell, as long as he was just standing there, he checked those papers in his coat pocket too. But he hadn't thought anyone would want to steal a few sheets of onionskin and some ugly photo-prints. So as soon as the gal said all her own stuff seemed to be there, he helped her to her feet and said, "I have to catch the short line up to Saddle Rock, ma'am. I see you got off here to transfer as well?"

She dimpled wistfully up at him, as if to prove great minds tended to run along the same channels, and confided, "I'm bound for the town of Buckeye, at the end of another railroad spur, I fear."

He bent over to pick up his Stetson as he gallantly replied, "It ain't a fate to be feared, ma'am. I've been through Buckeye and it ain't so bad."

So they parted friendly, with Longarm waiting until she was out of earshot before he murmured to his saddle, "Of all sad words of song or pen, the saddest are, 'It might have been!' Ain't that poetic as shit?"

The last leg of his afternoon journey seemed the longest as the Saddle Rock combination followed its single-line feeder tracks to the north-northwest in a sidewinding way through the uncertain country where the Front Range came down to a sea of grass. The High Plains seemed to almost beat in waves against a rocky shore, although they were moving mighty slowly if at all. Longarm spied ever more cows out yonder, grazing the short-grass swells between those ever bigger slabs of redrock sticking up out of the range at the same steep angle, like giant flatirons, or tombstones, carved from blood-soaked slate and sandstone. He knew that back in what his Indian pals called their Shining Times, there'd been more cottonwood and box elders in the deeper draws. Cows could play pure hell with most any tree shoots but chokecherry, willow, or mesquite, which you hardly ever saw on such high and dry range to begin with. Longarm had long since decided that, if he ever retired from the Justice Department and settled down like those pesky gals kept suggesting, he'd only run white-faced Hereford beef, and fence off any streams on his spread to give the natural flora and fauna an even break.

But he hadn't been sent all this way to tell folks they were overgrazing. So when the combination began to slow, he let the anxious cowboys crowd forward alone. He didn't see any Indians. That was no mystery. Recent trouble with the Ute and their Shoshoni cousins had reminded a lot of Colorado riders how they felt about Mister Lo, the poor Indian. Quill Indians of all the horse nations had learned to spook at the sight of a Stetson worn brim-level with its crown telescoped in the north range style. For most every white along the length of the old Goodnight-Loving Trail recalled how the Comanche had treated Captain Charlie Goodnight's sidekick, Oliver Loving, and how Cheyenne under Roman Nose had butchered and raped the cattle-raising Hungates south of Denver in country much the same as this.

A sudden wild consideration inspired Longarm to take out the sepia-tones of Deathless Dan Marlow. But as he studied the blankly staring features of the cuss from York State, he decided that lots of ugly white men had parrot noses jutting out of kite-shaped faces. It hardly mattered whether the long-dead Deathless Dan had been part Indian or not. What mattered was that he was dead and doubtless fairly decomposed by this time. Those other photographs he was still waiting to see had to be photographs of a . . . coincidence?

It was easy to buy some other gent entirely with a strong resemblance to a long-gone gunslick. That barber back in Denver who looked like the mortal twin of another dead outlaw was an obvious example. But then he was behaving like a barber instead of a bank robber. Whoever that schoolmarm and magazine photographer had caught on silver iodide on the dead killer's last stamping grounds seemed to be killing lawmen the same way the real Deathless Dan had.

Longarm put the pictures away again, muttering, "Not one two-gun man in a hundred holds both guns out in front of him to blaze away. It can't be Deathless Dan. But the son of a bitch knows he looks like him and he's going out of his way to imitate him!"

Then the train had stopped at the end of the line. So Longarm got up to carry his saddle the length of the coach and down to the sun-brightened open platform.

He wasn't surprised to spy young Nat Hayward and some others waiting for him. He wasn't even surprised by the mild changes in the kid's sort of friendly pup features. It stood to reason a man looked a few years older after you hadn't seen him for a few years.

As they shook hands, Nat asked if he'd brought the prints from his Denver files. Longarm nodded and replied, "Right here in my pocket. I'm fixing to wire Billy Vail the moment I compare 'em with those new prints of your own. You Western Union's still next to that one hotel, right?"

Nat nodded, but asked, "Ain't you seen the pictures of that spooky cuss we sent you, pard?"

Longarm said, "Reckon they're still in the mail, and Billy Vail is one of them fidgety old farts who want you to chop the winter's wood on April Fool's Day. You'd best let me see what you've got as we all traipse across to that Western Union."

But the young town law man said, "I just sent your boss *my* prints. They cost fifty cents apiece, and the town council is still arguing about whether I get a raise or not."

Longarm started to cloud up. But before he could say they

18

made *him* keep everything in triplicate, Hayward explained, "They got nigger-livers on glass, over to the photography studio."

When Longarm dryly asked if *negatives* might be what they were talking about, the kid nodded eagerly and explained, "That's what you call 'em. On glass. They tell me they can run off as many prints as I may or may not need. So why fill up drawers with four-bit pieces of fragile paper when Gordon's Gallery has every picture they ever took on fireproof glass? Come on. I'll show you. You remember how close it is from your last time, right?"

Longarm fell in step with the new town law and what seemed to be a couple of new deputies, but protested, "Hold on. This ain't no feather cushion I'm packing here. What say I run this baggage over to that hotel by the Western Union and hire a room. Seeing it's getting late in the day for train rides, it could save us running in circles if we split up to meet in, say, an hour at the Western Union?"

Hayward nodded. "How may of us would you have doing what? Do you want just copies of them recent pictures or a total set, starting with Deathless Dan on that cellar door?"

Longarm started to say one thing, then declared, "All the pictures ever taken, dead or alive, and ask 'em to focus them larger and sharper if they can. Did you say someone called Gordon is running that studio now? Whatever happened to those two French ladies I had to argue with the last time?"

Nat Hayward chuckled fondly. "They argued too much to stay in business in these parts. A less artisticated gent called Phil Gordon bought 'em out. Cheap. I reckon you'll find him willing to print your new copies black, white, or any color you want. He's got this immigrant gal who can color your portrait natural as anything, and she ain't half as snooty about it as them Demille gals were."

Longarm nodded. "In that case ask for their largest-size

19

prints in black and white. Meanwhile, could we have one of your deputies here rustle up Doc Kruger and tell him I need an exhumation permit from him, the local magistrate, or whoever?''

Nat Hayward blinked. ''I'd best handle that and have Ike here run over to the photographer. I reckon Doc Kruger has the final say on dead folks in these parts, him being our deputy coroner. I take it we are talking about another look at that coffin in that mausoleum over to the west?''

Longarm nodded. ''I'm surprised that never occurred to anyone in these parts earlier, no offense.''

Nat Hayward grinned sheepishly and confessed, ''I'm new at tracking down haunts. Do you mind if we ride out after supper? That body has been moldering out yonder close to three years, and I ain't looking forward to such a chore *before* I eat!''

Chapter 3

Longarm hired a room for the night at the one hotel in town, but had them put his saddle and bridle on a bay gelding at the livery across the way, explaining he'd be back for them directly.

Then he crossed over to the Western Union next to the hotel and used separate telegram blanks to compose nearly identical messages.

Noting the curious expression on the telegraph clerk's face, he explained, "I ride for a boss with the patience of a milk-starved baby boy. Meanwhile, as long as I'm still waiting for some answers, I've composed two wires. In essence, one says yes and the other says no. I'll know which one I want you to send in a minute, Lord willing and the old boys I'm to meet here don't get lost in the gathering darkness."

The clerk looked blank and allowed the sun hadn't set yet.

Longarm said it was about to, and added he meant to grab a bite to eat before he rode out to the graveyard. For some reason that made the clerk look confused.

The kid deputy they'd sent to the photographer came in about then. His name was Ike Something and he apologized for taking so long, explaining, "The boss had gone home for supper and

21

it took Miss Valya some time to set up them neggy twigs and delope these here prints. They got them a machine in their darkroom that runs electrical. Ain't that a bitch?''

Longarm held out his hand as he replied, ''We live in changing times, and that new Cheyenne Social Club has Edison lighting with its own steam-powered dynamo. Let's see what we've got here.''

He spread the fresh black and white prints the kid had handed him across the Western Union counter as the clerk craned for a look on the far side. Longarm put the smaller sepia-tone prints beside the older black and white views of the late Deathless Dan. He wasn't as surprised to see they matched as he was by the more recent views of what seemed to be the same son of a bitch alive and well.

As Billy Vail had said, one picture taken in sunlight out in front of a whitewashed schoolhouse showed a gaggle of grinning schoolkids with Deathless Dan or his twin brother off to one side, as if he'd stopped politely to avoid walking between the kids and the camera. From the expression on his parrot-beaked face he seemed to feel he was out of range of the camera.

The likeness was even clearer in an interior view, shot by flash powder, in the velvet-hung interior of Madame Laverne's house of ill repute. Deathless Dan was at the bar with others, looking just a tad annoyed, although not staring into the lens the way most of the others were. Longarm could picture someone shouting for everyone to hold still and then flashing his powder before anyone who didn't want his picture taken could get out of the way.

Longarm sighed and handed the message confirming the resemblance to the telegraph clerk, who scanned it and said, ''I see what you meant now. What's this about an exhumation order?''

Longarm said, ''Just send it the way I spelled it and my boss

22

will follow my drift if I spelled it wrong."

But young Ike wanted to know if exhumation meant digging up dead folks. So Longarm explained, "Only when they're buried, Ike. We only have to open some doors and coffin lids this evening."

Ike said, "Well, I can see for myself them pictures were took of the same cuss. I'll be switched with bobwire and sprinkled with salt before I'd say who they really put in that tomb with them dead whores. But whether we're talking about identical twins or some other confusion, you ain't going to be able to tell what the cadaver in that coffin was like in life. He's been rotting up on Signal Rise for close to three long years!"

As if to back Ike's play, Nat Hayward came in with his other kid deputy, Sid Marner, and the older Doc Kruger, who doubled as a deputy coroner for the county when he wasn't setting bones or lancing boils. Doc had been told what Longarm wanted, and had heard the last of Ike's argument. So he shook hands with Longarm, but agreed that a positive identification was likely to be a real chore after all this time.

Longarm said, "Mebbe. The body was embalmed and then shelved in a sandstone crypt at high altitude. Such thin dry air does a fair job of mummifying Indian cliff dwellers who were never embalmed, and like Ike says, it's barely been three years. Do you have the authority without a court order, Doc?"

Kruger sniffed and said, "I'm the highest authority on such matters as you'll get in these parts, with our circuit-riding county judge in Buckeye this week. We have to get the key to that mausoleum from the undertaker who embalmed the son of a bitch, seeing Madame Laverne left town without saying what she wanted done or not done with the fancy mausoleum she got cheap off a regular customer."

Longarm said that sounded as sensible as wasting time on a supper he didn't really feel like. So they all went outside. Longarm was the only one who had to run across the street to get his own mount. The others had all mounted the ponies in front of the telegraph office by the time he rejoined them aboard the bay.

Doc Kruger took the lead, knowing the way to the undertaker's house a tad upwind of the grim business establishment he ran. As Doc tersely explained, some bodies came in off the range a tad pungent with the spring thaw, and the undertaker's woman refused to serve meals or spend a night under the same roof with dead folks.

The undertaker, a jolly old elf called Herb Norman, came out to his gate to see what the sunset riders wanted, and not only offered to rustle up the key, but insisted on tagging along. He said he didn't want anyone busting things up, and confessed he was as curious as most kids his age would have been. He was about fifty, had lost count of the folks he'd embalmed, and hardly ever got to see any of them after such a time sealed away.

So there were six of them as they rode the few furlongs out to Signal Rise in the gloaming. Wanting as much expert opinion as he could get, Longarm managed to ride between the deputy coroner and the undertaker, with Nat Hayward and his kid deputies, Ike and Sid, leading the way.

Doc Kruger was of the opinion Deathless Dan Marlow had been as dead as one could possibly get, even before his autopsy. Old Herb Norman agreed it had struck him the same way, and added he hardly ever embalmed and boxed folks in any shape to stand around and have their pictures taken.

Longarm explained, "There's no doubt the three of us saw the same coffin lid nailed shut on the rascal I shot out behind that whorehouse. I didn't stay for the whole funeral. But you'll both recall I was at the autopsy with my own notebook handy. What I want to take down this time involves how close the real Deathless Dan resembled that rascal I still have to catch. I know they say the camera never lies. But that ain't always true and things look different in the flesh than in black and white on flat paper.''

Doc Kruger grimaced and said, ''Herb here would be the expert on how much flesh we're likely to see on a skull that was never too pretty to begin with!''

But the plump older undertaker shook his head and said, ''No, I'm not. That's why I wanted to ride along with the rest of you and see for myself. My customers keep surprising hell out of me. Maybe that's why I find my trade more interesting than my old woman does. I mind a time we had to ship the remains of a Mex cowhand back to his home in old Monterrey. Even though he'd only been in the ground less than eighteen months, there was hardly enough of him left to bother with. Yet other times, they hold together marvelously well. Might you recall that delicate business about Abe Lincoln's remains, Deputy Long?''

Longarm nodded soberly. ''I never got to work on that case. But it was federal and I saw the pictures. Eleven years after Lincoln had been laid to rest in Springfield, Illinois, a trio of desperados suffering from delusions of intelligence busted into the National Lincoln Monument and pried out Lincoln's coffin. They meant to hold it for a two-hundred-thousand-dollar ransom. But one of the gang, a Lewis Swegles, was really a Secret Service agent. He'd thought he was spying on some counterfeiters until they got really silly.''

Longarm glanced up as the last of the setting sun winked out behind the mountains to the west and continued. ''The arrest was made by a Captain Tyrell, and all of us were sore as hell when the two real crooks, Hughes and Mullen, were sentenced for no more than stealing a coffin worth seventy-five dollars. But what you're talking about was the identification of the coffin's contents, right?''

The undertaker nodded. ''I understand there was a lot of

discussion about that before they opened it up after eleven years.''

Longarm nodded soberly. ''There was. Some allowed it would be disrespectful. Others held they had to be certain Hughes and Mullen hadn't really been *at* the hallowed remains. So they pried off the lid and cut through the inner lining of lead foil, and there Honest Abe was, his face dark as saddle leather, which it *was* in a way, but otherwise intact enough to recognize from his photographs. They reburied him in a big old block of cement lest his coffin be stolen again. Seeing what fine shape he was in after eleven years, I reckon he'll just stay the same, like one of them Egyptian kings. But I was asking about Deathless Dan Marlow, Herb.''

The undertaker shrugged and replied, ''You've answered your very own question. We're not allowed to go as far as the ancient Egyptians these days. Our so-called embalming is only meant to keep things tidy long enough for a decent funeral. And two bodies buried side by side can go mighty separate ways. I just can't say what we're going to see when I remove the screws, not nails, from Dan Marlow's coffin lid. He could have wound up little more than soggy bones, or could seem ready to sit up and say howdy after this much time in a cool dry place. I've long suspected many a tale of saints, or vampires, was inspired by such odd cadavers. They say King Charlemagne was perfectly preserved when they moved his remains after hundreds of years. I forget why they wanted to move them or whether they thought he was a vampire or a saint. That's the gate to the Signal Rise Cemetery, just this side of those trees. I mean, there's *supposed* to be a gate, but the damned kids seem to find it amusing to ride off with 'em as fast as we can replace 'em.''

As they turned up the winding gravel path between dimly lit stone monuments great and small, Longarm idly asked if vandalism was that serious out there with nobody watching at night.

Herb Norman shrugged. "The little bastards have been content to steal the gate, or maybe a bench, or tip over a tombstone now and again. They know that if they really desecrated the grave of anyone important, they could wind up paying all out of proportion for the fun of their crime. We have stockmen in these parts who'd as soon hang a cow thief from a handy cottonwood as haul him into town for trial, and you'd make such riders even madder if you pestered their dead kin. That's Madame Laverne's mausoleum to your left, behind that marble angel missing one wing."

Longarm had his bearings now. As they reined in on the path lest a horse apple land on someone's grave, Nat Hayward called out in the forced joviality he felt the situation called for. "Are you fixing to stake out the back door whilst we pound on the front one, pard?"

Longarm had never seen a mausoleum that small with more than one entrance. But he could match stupid suggestions as well as anyone. So he soberly replied, "Good idea. Why don't you have your own boys do that this time? Far be it from me to hog all the glory when Deathless Dan makes a dash for his dead pony."

Nat Hayard just laughed as Sid Marner dismounted and called out, "Let's go, Ike. I mind a swell place to cover the back of this big box from."

Herbe Norman snorted, "Kids! Mind you don't trample any flowers out back, boys!"

Then he was off his own pony and moving toward the fair-sized solid door of weathered bronze, set in dark scab-colored sandstone cut from the prevalent bedrock of the surrounding foothills. He led the way with his key ring and a bull's-eye lantern, muttering dry comments about back doors, for God's sake.

As Longarm, Doc Kruger, and Nat Hayward crowded closer, the undertaker turned the key, but seemed to be hauling on the bronze door handle without a whole lot of luck. So Longarm offered to give it a try, and took over to put his own stronger back into it.

The door seemed stuck solid, until something gave and Longarm and the door swung wide to almost crash into the sandstone wall. Then the undertaker let go of his lantern as someone *inside* started blasting away through the open doorway!

Longarm let go of the door handle and hit the graveyard grass as he drew his .44-40 and trained it on the oblong black opening. He could smell the gunsmoke better than he could see it as it drifted from the darkness in the ruby light of the late gloaming. Herb Norman's lantern had gone out, but the undertaker sounded all right as he gasped, "What in the hell was that? Sounded like those pesky kids rigged up some fireworks inside!"

From further out on the grass Doc Kruger called, "That wasn't any firecracker that Nat here stopped! I make it a .44 or .45. We'll know better as soon as we get him to my dispensary!"

"Everyone move out of line from yonder doorway!" Longarm called in an urgent tone as he heard Nat Hayward weakly declare, "It's only a flesh wound. I'm getting my breath back and we got to *get* the son of a bitch! So let me up, Doc!"

Kruger insisted, "I'll be the judge of how you feel, you fool kid! Would at least one of you help me get Nat back aboard his pony?"

Sid Marner rounded one corner of the mausoleum and called out, "What's up? We heard gunshots just now!"

Longarm called back, "You did. Cover the back tight whether you see a back door or not." Then, as the kid deputy crawfished away in the gloom, Longarm called to the undertaker, "Herb, you'd better help with Nat. The rest of us have to keep the one who shot him in that box till he sees the light and surrenders, or till it's light enough to go in after him! This child ain't about to give him another shot as easy as the one he just put into Nat!"

Chapter 4

It felt as if he'd been belly down in the grass with his six-gun trained on the gaping door of the mausoleum for the whole night by the time Doc and Herb got back with at least a platoon of riders from town to back their play.

It had really been more like an hour and a half, and in the meantime Longarm had circled some to relight the undertaker's lantern and set it atop a handy tombstone with its bull's-eye beam trained into the gaping doorway of the silent mausoleum.

The others could see what he intended as they dismounted at safe distances and crept in to join him. Longarm asked Doc Kruger how Nat Hayward was making out.

The deputy coroner hunkered down in the grass beside him to say, "Nat and me were both right. It was a flesh wound in his right hip, and the slug I dug out of him was a .45 with a strong family resemblance to the ones I dug out of poor Constable Crabtree the other evening. Nat's resting comfortably at my place, with his own wife and mine to comfort him. I brought something back that might smoke that other cuss out."

Longarm asked what was in the brown pint bottle the medical man held in one hand. Doc Kruger explained, "Spirits of ammonia and formaldehyde. I've yet to meet a mere mortal who could stand the stink of either in a poorly ventilated room.''

Longarm chuckled like a mean little kid and said, "Would you care to do the honors or shall I, seeing it was your evil notion.''

Kruger laughed as meanly and handed Longarm the bottle, explaining that he'd never played baseball all that well as a kid.

Longarm shifted his shooting iron to his left hand as he took the hefty brown bottle, calling out loud enough to be heard around to the back, "Everybody look sharp and aim low as the son of a bitch makes his move. I am about to feed him some stink he'll find fatal if he stays in there breathing it!''

Then he wound up and threw, dropping back down as they all heard the crash of shattering glass on the stone floor inside.

Nothing happened for a spell. Then Longarm sniffed and marveled, "Jesus H. Christ, you can smell that hellish mixture all the way out here! Could I have a medical opinion on the effects on anyone inside right now, Doc?''

Kruger grimaced and said, "He might have killed himself with the last of those shots we heard earlier. I don't think anyone would be able to choose death by ammonia and formaldehyde inhalation if they wanted to. Not without coughing a lot at least.''

Longarm said, "I follow your drift. My eyes are watering clean out here in the open air. But he's got to be in there, Doc. The light ain't *that* dim, and the more I think back to other such structures, the surer I get that there's no other way in or out.''

As they just went on staring at the henhouse-sized stone structure, the undertaker on Longarm's other side declared in an even surer tone, "There isn't even a roof vent. Bugs and bats get in unless you seal a mausoleum almost airtight. I like the doc's suggestion he shot Nat and then killed himself. Don't ask me why. Nobody with a rational mind would be acting so

31

crazy. I know what even my old woman says about my family trade. But as accustomed to the dead as I may be, you'd never find me living in a crypt with dead whores and gunslicks!''

Doc Kruger suggested, ''What if he wasn't living in there? What if he just knew we were coming out this way and headed us off, to ambush Nat the way he just did?''

Longarm thought before he quietly asked, ''How could anyone know I was going to drag Nat out here tonight? And then, assuming he must have, why would anyone go to this much trouble and back himself into such a trap, just to gun a lawman he could have gunned in town as easily as he gunned Constable Crabtree?''

The undertaker said, ''I don't think he was after our town law. At the risk of turning your pretty little head, Longarm, I think he was after you. You would have been smack in the doorway with my bull's-eye lantern outlining you if you hadn't been bossing that stubborn door around!''

Longarm nodded soberly. ''I should have thanked you for that favor earlier. As *I* think back, any number of gossips might have known they were sending me up from Denver, and I've been jawing all over town about coming out here for a look-see at that dead body inside. Did you ever get the feeling somebody was trying to keep you from looking at something, Herb?''

The jovial undertaker replied, ''Happens all the time in my trade. Folk are always winding up dead in ridiculous positions, and you have no idea how much trouble some kin will go to to keep certain secrets in the family. I mind this one time a sweet old spinster screwed herself to death with a broom handle and—''

''I think that crypt may have aired out enought for a closer look,'' Longarm said, asking the professional on his other side, ''Is it safe to try, Doc?''

Kruger grimaced and replied, ''I told you I just dug a two-hundred-and-thirty-grain slug out of Nat Hayward's right hip. But on the other hand, I don't think anyone could have inhaled those fumes just now if they were alive when you heaved my little bottle.''

Longarm left the bull's-eye lantern exposed where it was as he got up and moved in out of line of anyone inside the door. As he flattened his back against the red sandstone to the right of the door with his gun in line with his head, the reek of pungent chemicals was tough to take, even outside in the open. Longarm called out, ''We know you're in there. Come out with your hands polite and we'll talk about what's ailing you, old son.''

There was no reply. He hadn't really expected any. There wasn't a thing he could do but wait a spell for the fumes to clear some more, then drop to his belly again and risk a peek around the bottom of the doorjamb, like a gnome hoping to surprise an ogre with a bead on the door at waist level.

There didn't seem to be an ogre or anyone else alive in the small stone chamber. The bull's-eye beam was shining in over Longarm's head to light up the interior well enough. He spied three coffins against as many blank walls, all at ground level. He wasn't as worried about how they might have planned for later interments as he was about armed elves behind those coffins. There didn't seem to be room for anyone bigger to be hiding behind them.

He rose and called back to the others, ''Empty. Or so it seems. Did you say you could open these coffins gently, Herb?''

The undertaker rose and moved forward, cheerfully calling back, ''I screwed all three of those boxes shut. I'd be proud to show you how to unscrew the lids. But you're not going to like this, old son.''

Herb joined Longarm in the doorway, along with Doc Kruger and Sid Marner, who said Ike Baker was still out back and that no damned nothing had sneaked through no damned stone walls.

Longarm asked which box they'd put Deathless Dan in. He wasn't too surprised to hear the dead killer had been shoved against a wall a tad closer to the door. But he suggested, "Let's start with that one against the back wall, Herb. That solid mahogany offers fair cover, and a sneak popping up like a jack-in-the-box would have a better shot out this one door."

Herb shrugged and said, "I don't care which one we start with. None of 'em are likely to look pretty. Lord have mercy if I don't prefer the smell of death to that damned ammonia, though. Somebody fetch that lantern and let's see if more light doesn't help."

Sid Marner ran out to fetch the lantern as Longarm lit a wax Mexican match and held it aloft above the rear coffin.

Norman said, "Nobody's been popping up out of this box. Can't you see how corroded those brass screws are? They called her Snake Hips, and we listed the cause of death as abusive drinking, complicated by the clap and consumption."

Longarm held his .44-40 politely but ready down at his side as he quietly said, "Open it up and let's have a look anyway."

So Norman got to work with his pocket screwdriver, muttering about how tight the screws were as Sid Marner came in with that far brighter lantern before Longarm had to strike another Mex match.

They were sort of sorry Sid had done that when Herb Norman raised the lid just long enough to quietly ask, "Satisfied?"

When Longarm gasped, "You can shut that box again!" the undertaker did so, tersely explaining, "The fat ones puddle like that as their lard goes rancid. Poor thing had been proud of that pink dress, and now look at it. But at least the smell ain't so bad, thanks to my chemistry and the four years she's had to marinate. You want to see what shape Dan Marlow's in now?"

Longarm pointed his chin at the other whore's coffin as he

said, "Why don't we save the good stuff for last. Was that one in here the day you brought Marlow's remains to such cheerful surroundings?"

Norman stepped over to the other coffin and bent to start working on its lid as he replied, "It was. Funny how two of Madame Laverne's working girls died the same year she opened for business here in such a healthy climate. The madam got this crypt at a bargain, and I gave her a good price on them boxes, figuring she might be a steadier customer. But nary a whore ever died on us since then. Doc Kruger there sure must know his oats."

Longarm turned to the town's only doctor, at least as far as he knew, but before he could speak, Kruger drew himself up and snapped, "Whores have as much right to medical treatment as anyone else. And it was my Christian duty to examine the whole crew once a month for the good of the community. Would you want some townsman or stockman carrying the clap home to his wife?"

Longarm shook his head and said, "I never intended to make moral judgments, Doc. I was about to ask if what Herb said was true. Are the two of you telling me it was possible to run a whorehouse in a trail town for four whole years without anyone getting sick or hurt?"

Herb Norman said, "This one died after she fell down the stairs. Or so they said."

As he opened the coffin to reveal little more than a skeleton held together by shreds of dry skin and a black silk dress, Kruger said, "Damn it, I ruled that death accidental because there was no evidence anyone pushed her down those stairs, even though it was a Saturday night when the herds were in town. As for her sisters in sin, I've lost count of the number of agues and injuries I was called on to treat over those mysterious four years. There could be something to the notion of our thin dry air being healthy. For those girls would drink, cuss, and pull one another's hair. But what was I supposed to do, let them die when they were sick or hurt?''

Longarm said, "Don't get your bowels in an uproar, Doc. I know neither you nor the late Constable Crabtree could have run them all out of town without orders from your city council. I know how city councils deal with discreet and profitable vice too. Let's say no more about it and have a look at the cuss who's been credited—or was it blamed—for chasing all them whores away.''

Herb Norman shut the dead whore's lid and moved over to the last coffin as Longarm added absently, "Could anybody tell me just when that happened? I know you say someone who looked like Deathless Dan did the deed and then shot Crabtree when he was called on it, but . . .''

Doc Kruger answered. "I don't think the constable was fussing with his killer about running Madame Laverne out of town. I know for a fact he didn't approve of her or her gals. Albeit you're so right about municipal tax rolls.''

Longarm kept his gun aimed politely at the stone floor, ready to aim most anywhere, as he watched Norman working on the last of the screws while Doc Kruger added, "I think Constable Crabtree only wanted to know who in thunder a man who looked like a dead killer might be. And why he'd been photographed in Madame Laverne's just a day or so before she and all her girls vanished into thin air.''

Longarm blinked and said, "I reckon I'd have wanted to ask the same sort of questions. But how come you say a day or *so*? Can't anybody be more specific?''

Kruger said, "That old whore and her crew moved out in the middle of the week, late at night, with neither customers nor neighbors to say for sure whether it was a Wednesday or a Thursday. Nobody really noticed until some cowhands rode in of a Saturday afternoon to get laid and wound up mighty chagrined.''

Longarm didn't care. He lost interest in the casual conversation about missing whores when Norman raised the coffin lid to show them all that Madame Laverne and her gals weren't the only ones missing.

There came a collective gasp from everyone crowded around before Herb Norman almost sobbed, "I don't understand this at all! There was almost a hundred and sixty pounds of cadaver in here the last time I screwed that lid down!"

Doc Kruger asked for more light as they all stared down into the empty coffin. It had been lined with ivory-colored artificial silk, padded with wood shavings. You could tell because, aside from being empty, the interior of the once-handsome coffin was a mite torn and messy. Someone asked what all that dried crud on the bottom was, and Herb Norman explained, "We do our best, but there's always some ooze as decomposition sets in. What you see there is nothing to what you'd get in damper air with no embalming."

Someone said, "I rode too close to an Arapaho sky burial one day. That old Indian was dripping like a sugar maple in February. Only it didn't smell as nice."

Longarm didn't care about other dead folks. He was already outside and whipping around to the back, calling out, "We seem to be missing someone that must have been inside, dead or alive, when he put a round in Nat Hayward this evening. Anyone back here see anyone passing through stone walls recently?"

Ike Baker called back, "I've been right here ahint this angel since we rid out here, and I ain't seen shit. How could anyone have been in that big stone box with a pistol-gun if he ain't there now?"

To which Longarm could only reply, "Damn it. I just said that!"

Chapter 5

They wasted the better part of an hour proving there were no secret openings in the simple but well-mortared sandstone mausoleum. More than one of the men from town made uneasy mention of the way Constable Crabtree's killer had sort of faded away by the time anyone could look for him seriously. Others who joshed that they didn't believe in haunts sounded just as uneasy.

Herb Norman finally locked up and they all rode back to town in the moonlight, laughing too loud at owl hoots and other night noises all about.

At Doc Kruger's dispensary they found Nat Hayward still alive but dead to the world as his wife sat by his cot to hold his hand and he slept off the heroic dose of laudanum the doc confessed to giving him earlier.

Laudanum was a mixture of alcohol and opium. Kruger showed Longarm why he'd used so much as they stepped back out into his examination and treatment room. There was still some blood on the big blob of lead and some slivers of bone in a tin bowl on the sideboard. Kruger said he hadn't had time to tidy up yet, and added, "It looks just like the rounds we found in Constable Crabtree during his autopsy. The .45-28s made by Schofield Arms, right?''

Longarm shook his head and declared, ''More likely Frankford Armory. Schofield ain't a brand. It's more like a notion an army ordinance officer called Schofield had a few years back. His design made it a tad easier to reload under fire. He ordered pistols made to his specs from Smith and Wesson, Colt, Remington, and anyone else who wanted to run off a gross or so. But in the end the army went with the Colt '74 because it didn't fall apart as easy in the hands of a recruit. That put lots of fair .45s on the market cheap.''

He raised the tin bowl to the light and squinted as he decided, ''.45-caliber for certain. Need its brass to even guess at the make and powder charge. You dug these bone splinters from the same wound?''

Kruger nodded. ''I had to. They were in there. Nat got off lucky. Only one of the two rounds we heard hit him, and he took it through nothing but meat until it hit his ilium at just the right angle.''

Longarm nodded and said, ''That ilium would be what the rest of us call the hipbone. So these slivers were chipped off as the bullet came to rest, right?''

Kruger nodded. ''An inch lower and he'd have been lamed for life, assuming I could have saved a leg with a shattered hip socket. What does this have to do with the identity of the one who shot him, Deputy Long?''

Longarm shrugged. ''Likely nothing. I follow your drift about inches either way. One shot missed entire, meaning the shooter wasn't the greatest marksman ever born. The one as hit could've hit his hip socket, as you just said, or hurt him even worse by taking him through his bladder or balls the other way. So I doubt anyone could have been just funning.''

Kruger's jaw dropped and he gasped, ''My God! Are you suggesting Nat Hayward could have been in cahoots with the man who just came within inches of killing him?''

Longarm put the tin bowl aside and reached for a cheroot as he confided, ''The thought had crossed my mind. Lord knows when they'd have ever promoted Nat if Crabtree had gone on living. By the way, how many of you Saddle Rock officials are standing for re-election come November?''

Doc Kruger said, ''We elect our mayor and board of aldermen, or city council. They in turn appoint lesser lights such as the late Constable Crabtree. I was appointed deputy coroner by the county down in Fort Collins, before you ask.''

Longarm smiled thinly and said, ''Wasn't about to. I'm paid to *know* how such government cogs mesh, Doc. I knew deputy coroners, undersheriffs, and such were confirmed by the county board of supervisors, making you a piss-poor suspect with nothing to gain by conspiring to have a town official assassinated by a spook. So I'd best light this smoke outside and see about scouting up that spook, or my supper leastways.''

They shook on it and parted friendly. Longarm rode the hired bay back to the livery, left his saddle and such in their tack room, and headed across to his hotel with his saddlebags and Winchester.

He was glad he'd hired that hotel room now, seeing it was going on ten-thirty and they'd about rolled the walks up for the night in Saddle Rock.

He stored his possibles in his second-story room before he asked the sleepy-looking night clerk whether this hotel had a restaurant that might still be serving.

The clerk snorted in disgust and confided they didn't have such a big-city notion on the premises in broad daylight. Then he relented enough to suggest, ''Cattle outfit camped out back. We rent our spare lot out to such outfits when they pass through here. I know for sure they were making coffee, at least, less than an hour ago. The good old trail boss sent a cup of Arbuckle and some sourdough biscuits in to tide me over, Lord love 'em.''

Longarm told the older clerk he deserved to be loved a heap too, then mosied outside to circle the frame hotel until, sure enough, he could see a chuck wagon, a remuda of tethered ponies, and a bunch of riders seated or reclining around a night fire in the center of the two-acre lot. He knew that as long as anyone was still awake in a cow camp a visitor rated a cup of coffee and at least some biscuits.

Visiters were well advised to stay the hell away from a cow camp after everyone but the proddy night guard was bedded down for the night. That might have been why the outfit had elected to bed down smack in town. They didn't seem to have any herd with them.

As Longarm strode in, someone around the fire must have mentioned it. A figure rose, outlined by the firelight, to silently await his approach to within explaining range. It was easy to see the good old trail boss had to be a mighty well-built woman, even if she was wearing jeans, a man's shirt, and a gun slung low on one hip.

Her Carlsbad Stetson, outlined from behind, looked familiar. She had the greater advantage of facing away from the fire as he walked into its glow with his bare face hanging out. So she was the one who broke the ice with; "Custis Long, you hard-riding asshole, what in thunder are you doing up this way?"

Longarm grinned back and replied, "I was about to ask you the same less crudely, Miss Edwina. I was wondering what a cow outfit was doing here in town with the fall roundup almost over."

When she told him she was on a buying ride, and invited him to stay and have some late supper, he quickly agreed. For he knew Edwina Chaffee from the Holy Cross Trail, although not in any biblical sense, since there had been riders all around at every infernal trail break.

Edwina Chaffee, despite her jeans and the way she could ride and rope, was more a businesswoman than a cowgirl. Raised in the cattle business so she knew it from the ground up, then backed by kissing-cousin Chaffees in the banking and mining business, Edwina had given up raising her own cows in favor of buying beef on the hoof to herd over into the high country of Colorado, where hardrock miners made three times as much as mill hands and wanted steak and potatoes on the table when they came off shift. The petite but athletic Edwina enjoyed a rep for being honest in her dealings but rough on cow thieves. She had no rep either way as a single gal who was getting a mite long in the tooth for pure virginity. She didn't act scared of men. She was inclined to cuss worse than some of them. On the other hand, if she'd been screwing any of her riders that time he'd ridden over to the west slope from Leadville with the outfit, Longarm hadn't been able to tell.

They sat him down and served him black coffee and sourdough biscuits with his son-of-a-bitch stew. He could tell they'd added onions to the marrow-gut, kidneys, and such. He was glad he'd waited for supper, and he said so. So then he had to tell them what he'd been up to at that graveyard earlier.

Edwina said she didn't believe in ghosts either. But the older gent who'd cooked the swell stew allowed it paid to have an open mind. He said, "I've never seen a haunt my ownself. But a heap of folk say they have and how do you account for that?"

Longarm washed down a lump of suet and quietly replied, "I reckon they were mistaken or lying. I know for a fact that folks lie all the time. I find that easier to buy than something downright impossible!"

Another hand asked, "How can you be sure haunts ain't possible, if so many others say they've seen 'em?"

Longarm snorted, "I just now told you all what I thought of the word of a self-confessed pagan. If man or beast was able to traipse about as dead meat, dry bones, or that wispy protoplasm that just ain't there, none of *us* would need to have hearts, lungs, or other innards to keep us going. It's all the way Professor Darwin says in that book he wrote just before the war. If a critter as insubstantial as a jellyfish aims to go any faster, it has to evolve itself eyes and a backbone. If it was possible to get by as something thinner than jelly, nature would have never gone to the trouble of evolving anything.''

The cook made a wry face and said, ''I don't hold with that Darwin fella. The Good Book was good enough for my grandad and it's good enough for me. It says right in Kings Two how Saul met witches and ghosts in that town of Endor!''

Longarm nodded and replied, ''That's how come anyone who brags on a hobby like that has to be a self-confessed pagan. Messing around like that is forbidden to folks of the Christian, Hebrew, or Moslem persuasion. Don't you recall how sore the Lord got at King Saul for pestering the dead who'd come to visit with *Him*?''

Edwina laughed and said, ''Saul wanted the spirit of Judge Samuel to advise him about that battle he was about to have with those Philistines. What's a Philistine anyway, Custis?''

Longarm said, ''Something like an ancient Greek, only different. In any case, the Good Book tells how the spirit appeared, all filled with righteous wrath, to cuss Saul out for pestering him after he'd died and earned his danged rest. Then Saul got killed in that battle the next day to teach him a good lesson. I've often suspected folks who dabble in that spiritualist stuff started by the Fox sisters in York State know they're not in any such danger and . . . Now ain't that *interesting,* as soon as you study on it!''

Edwina asked what he meant. He explained. ''All the current guff about protofuzz and financial advice from the spirit world hails from back around '48 in a gloomy house outside of Rochester, New York. Some schoolgals called Kate and Maggie Fox started scaring folks with odd rappings or joint poppings they blamed on a Mister Splitfoot from the Great Beyond. They should of been ashamed of themselves, but they weren't and they ain't. They're still holding seances back East for the likes of poor old Mary Todd Lincoln and other crazy ladies. What I just found so interesting is that the Fox sisters ain't the only products of Rochester, New York. That's where the Eastman Company makes cameras and photograph plates, speaking of spooky photographs I've been shown here in Saddle Rock!''

Nobody seemed to follow his drift but the canny Edwina, who nodded soberly and said, ''I've heard tell of trick photography, and that firm you just mentioned would know better than I whether they sell trick cameras that take pictures of haunts. But how do you account for the gunplay out at that graveyard this evening, Custis?''

To which he could only reply, ''I can't. What we saw was impossible under the natural laws of this world as I understand them. So we must have seen something else, or I just didn't understand what I thought I was seeing.''

He washed down the last of his hearty stew with the last of their fine coffee and continued. ''Come morning, I mean to go back over them photographs, the logical and the less so, with the folks who took them as well as the ones who developed them. For someone pulled some almost lethal stage magic on us this evening, and a cuss who could shoot two lawmen and just vanish into thin air might find it just as easy to have his photograph taken when he wasn't really there!''

Edwina repressed a shudder, but sounded enthusiastic when she told him, ''Me and the boys would sure like to track this Deathless Dan down with you, Custis. But we're moving down the Goodnight Trail with a view to gathering strays that escaped the market drives we've been having in these parts. If only I can gather six or eight hundred head before the passes snow shut, I have a standing order for that much beef in Durango.''

Longarm whistled and decided, ''That's a far drive for this

late in the year, Miss Edwina. I've seen it snow on the west slope as early as a couple of weeks ago. Indian summer don't hang on as long, once you get up above, say, seven thousand feet."

She snorted impatiently. "Tell me about driving cows over the Continental Divide, Custis. I've only been doing it for a living. We're not leaving tonight, though. Meeting a stockman in the morning with a dozen-odd yearlings his roundup crew missed. Where did you say you meant to spend the night your ownself?"

Longarm considered his options, decided truth had many things to be said for it, and confided, "I'm checked into that hotel yonder. I sleep on grass as sound as most, I reckon. But given my druthers, I'd as soon try a big old brass bedstead for a change."

It worked. In a desperately casual voice, Edwina Chaffe declared a lady with delicate bones might enjoy such a change. Then she quickly added, "That's if they still have a room for me to check into on my own, of course. Do you reckon they might, Custis?"

Longarm sounded as calm, he hoped, as he casually observed, "Well, that room clerk did say he enjoyed the coffee and biscuits you sent in to him earlier. Why don't we just go ask?"

So they did, with Edwina walking beside him as if butter wouldn't melt in her mouth. Just outside the last of the firelight she told him in a less innocent tone, "I've been dying to ask about you and that redhead who rode sidesaddle over on the Holy Cross Trail. What was her name, Miss Dragging Ass? Sounds like a fool Indian name if you ask me!"

He hadn't asked her. He knew she knew who Clara Drakmanton was. But he owed it to a swell pal as well as the richest gal around Lake County to keep some sweet secrets secret.

Not answering always seemed to inspire some gals to talk

bolder. So Edwina asked right out, "Well, damn it, did you or didn't you?"

It usually slowed them down when you asked them to spell out just what they were asking. But when he casually asked just what she thought he might have done with the beautiful society lady, the roughly dressed Edwina replied just as casually, "Did you screw her or not? You know how sore I was when you left me standing there in my chaps like a big-ass bird in that mining camp whilst you went chasing after all that henna-rinsed hair and fake silk. So what happened when you caught up with her? I had to get back to Leadville, like I told you."

Longarm stopped, swung her around to slam her against the front of his tweed suit, and planted a good kiss on her, making her grab for her hat, before he took his tongue back out of her mouth and growled down into her startled moonlit eyes, "You told me you were leaving and I let you. Just like I was fixing to do tonight. If you want men chasing after you instead of other ladies, you have to quit telling 'em you aim to leave *poco tiempo*!"

Then he kissed her some more.

When they came up for air she gasped, "I reckon I could stay just long enough to do that a few more times, Custis. But can I trust you to respect my purity, or at least not to blab all over if I let you have just a little feel?"

He chuckled and said, "You just tried to get me to gossip about another lady. That ain't my style. It ain't my style to settle for kid games either. You're the one who brought up screwing. I didn't think you wanted to when we parted friendly that other time. If you ain't ready to act like a grown woman instead of a schoolmarm in a porch swing, just say so and we'll part the same way tonight."

She said, "I have to book a separate room. One of my hands might ask. But I reckon I can show you a thing or two about

46

acting like any fancy flirt who rides sidesaddle!''

So he kissed her some more, cupping a denim-clad buttock in each palm to see if he could scare her off, and then they went around to the front, told the clerk the lady wanted a room of her own down the hall from his, and then went up to slam doors loud and ease them open softly a few minutes later.

Before Longarm took her in his arms again in the darkness of his own room he'd naturally gotten rid of his hat, coat, vest, and gunbelt. He could tell she'd left everything but her jeans and sateen shirt in her own room to run down the hallway to him barefoot.

But when he started to shift her toward the bed she protested she liked her own room better. She explained it was further from the stairs and closer to the running water in the ladies' bath down that way. So he just picked her up and said, ''Grab my gunbelt as we pass it on our way to paradise, Angel Lips.''

So she did, and he kicked the door shut behind them to sneak her along the dark corridor as she giggled fit to bust and insisted he'd done this sort of thing before.

He had, but he never said so as he dropped her across her own bed, hung his gun next to hers on the bedpost by the headboard, and made sure her door was bolted before he turned to see by the moonlight's dappled rays through the lace curtains that she was already peeling out of those jeans and that shirt, and that he'd been right about her not bothering with underwear in Indian summer.

As he sat down beside her to haul off his own boots, Edwina perched on her folded bare limbs and arched her spine to thrust her perky cupcakes proudly as she demurely asked if Clara Drakmanton's bare body was any better than her own.

It would have given away too much to say the two of them were built entirely different, Lord love 'em both. So he just said, ''I was as stuck for answers over in that mining camp, come to study on it, until a childishly simple answer came to me. I was trying to see why a tinhorn gambler I'd caught cheating kept losing card games on purpose. As soon as I saw he wasn't losing his own money the rest was simple. So tell me, why would a dead and forgotten killer want the law to know he was up and about again, even if he was?''

She pouted. ''I don't want to hear ghost stories. I want you to tell me why you ignored me to go after that other woman, damn it!''

He finished hauling down his pants, shucked his shirt even faster, and fell back across the bed with her to part the fuzz between her strong horsewomanly thighs and find her clit was already drooling as he strummed a sprightly banjo tune and kissed her some more.

She kissed him back, spreading her thighs and gripping his wrist to slow his banjo-plucking down as she protested, ''Don't tease me that way, Custis. Lay back and let me show you what I really want!''

So he rolled on his back bemused, as the curvy but firmly muscled little gal rolled upright, forked a thigh across him, and impaled her lust-gushed privates on his raging erection and they both gasped, ''Jeeeee-zusss!''

She bounced hard and hot, sobbing with desire, as he thrust up to meet her, until he suddenly came, sooner than he'd expected or meant to. He said he was sorry, and told her to keep going as she hunkered over him, gasping for breath with her love muscles milking the last of it out of him.

Then she said, ''I came too. Do you have a match, darling?''

He blinked and said, ''In my shirt pocket on the post, along with some fair smokes, if that's what you have in mind.''

She said it wasn't as she groped for the light without letting go of his throbbing organ-grinder. She explained she wanted to light the bed lamp and watch in the mirror as they did it some more.

He chuckled up at her and said, ''I was wondering what

48

you'd been up to down at this end of the hall. You adjusted yonder mirror before you invited me into this bedstead, right?''

She had to strain some to light the lamp without getting off him. The view was swell as she demurely replied, ''You've no idea how I've thought about this since you got away from me on the western slope and let me ride all those miles with a thwarted pussy rubbing on an indifferent saddle with my legs spread this wide. I just *knew* it would feel grand to ride this more romantic way. Albeit I never dreamt it could feel this good. Oh, look, I can see us in that mirror and you're fucking me, you dreadful man!''

Longarm laughed and declared, ''You ain't seen nothing yet if a *show* is what you're after.''

She said she was. So he rolled her off, posed her on her hands and knees, and moved around so she could see them from the side as he rammed it in and out of her dog-style. She arched her spine and waved her head wildly to lash the air with her sun-streaked brown hair as she moaned, ''Oh, Dear Lord! It looks so big and it feels so good and I've always known critters were enjoying it when they went at it this way. I look like a bitch dog being humped in the street and I love it! Hump me harder, Custis. Hump me till somebody has to come out and pour water over us to get us apart!''

He laughed and said he'd sure enjoy being hung up like that in such a pretty little puppy. He said it would take more than a pail of water to make him stop. But while water was one thing, fire was more frightening. So even though he was pounding away in her as hard as he could, he still sniffed deep and declared, ''I think I smell something burning. Do you?''

She moaned, ''Harder! Faster! Of course you smell something burning, you big oaf. You just lit that oil lamp and the wick may be a tad overdue for trimming. Don't you dare pull your wick out of me if you don't want my fire to go out!''

He didn't, until he heard someone clanging a fire-alarm triangle somewhere in the near distance. That was when he sniffed harder, took it out of her, and wistfully announced, "We're going to have to just hold the thought for now, Miss Edwina. This infernal hotel seems to be on fire!"

Chapter 6

Longarm knew he was right as soon as he felt the door, found it reasonably cool to the touch, and opened it to find the hall reeking with the stench of burning feathers and linen. He slammed the door shut again and told Edwina, "Smells like some other guest was smoking in bed."

He strapped his gun rig on over his hastily donned pants as he told her, "I'm going to make a run for my own hat, coat, and vest whilst you finish dressing. Don't try to leave without me. It may be safe to use the stairs. But I'll let you know for certain when I get back!"

Then he took a deep breath, slipped out in the blue haze, and shut the door after him before he ran for his own door without breathing.

His eyes were still watering by the time he grabbed the knob of a door he didn't recall locking, found it locked, and then, just as he recalled leaving the damned key in his damned coat inside, found a key in the door on the hall side, locking his hired room from the *outside*!

He twisted it and turned the knob. He opened the door to let out a thunderhead of billowing smoke, lit from behind by a hellish amber glow. So he slammed the door shut again just as two gents with red suspenders over their dark shirts and leather helmets on their heads came up the stairs, demanding, "Where's the fire?"

Longarm risked a breath, coughed, and gasped, "Right behind this door. Don't take any chances, boys. There's nobody in there with the blaze and it's a real pisser!"

They said they'd be the judge of that, and proceeded to smash the door in with their axes, even though it was unlocked. Longarm figured that had something to do with the amount of draft they wanted, unless they were just having fun. Being a volunteer fireman in a small town could get tedious, he'd been told.

He moved back down the hall to Edwina's room to tell her what was going on. That lamp was still burning. So there was no doubt Edwina had lit out, hat, spurs, and all.

He didn't care. He'd told her not to do that. But he could see how a gal might be more concerned for her reputation than burns on her still-reputable ass. He was just as glad he wouldn't be stuck with explaining such matters himself. He knew he was stuck with explaining something to somebody. The fire had started in his room of record. They were going to want to know how. He wanted to know a mite more than he did about that. He was sure he hadn't left anything lit in there before he'd swept out with Edwina in his arms.

From the jovial shouts down the hall and out front in the street, Longarm figured something encouraging had to be going on. So he strode down the other way to be told by a fireman stepping through his busted-up doorway, "Mattress and bedding were burning like hell, and neither the buckets of water nor sand we had with us seemed to help. So we throwed it all out the window and let the boys down below deal with it. No other damage, save for smoke and water stains. You know whose room that was?"

Longarm soberly replied, "Mine. I was down the hall, ah,

washing my hands, when . . . my mattress, you say?''

The second volunteer came out to nod absently at Longarm and tell his partner, ''Just figured why that window was already busted when we got inside. One of the boys down in the street thinks that mattress was soaked with Greek fire and that was why it was so tough to put out!''

Longarm didn't ask what Greek fire was. They'd used it, or at least they'd gotten as close to the old formula as they could, during the trench fighting around Petersburg near the end of the war. The nasty mixture of naptha, quicklime, and phosphorus burned on water to make mighty serious fire-bombs.

Seeing the smoke was thining out in the cross-ventilation, Longarm stepped into his ruined room to gather his hat, coat, and vest before he picked up his sooty saddlebags to follow the firemen downstairs.

He didn't put on anything but the hat. The brown tweed seemed to have made it through with no visible damage. But it smelled like a cremated buzzard. When he asked one of the firemen if there was a cleaner in town, he was told, ''Sure, come morning. Across from the municipal corral. You left all this stuff unguarded when you stepped out to take a crap, you say?''

Longarm nodded and quietly replied, ''I was in a hurry. I've read those signs telling me to watch my hat and coat. But there are risks we just have to take if we aim to get through life faster than a blamed turtle. I naturally keep my gun, my badge, and spending money on me at all times. Anyone who can steal my well-worn duds and spare socks are welcome to 'em if they really want to take such a risk of their own. How many sneak thieves would you reckon I had on my trail, waiting to swoop down the moment my back was turned?''

They were in the lobby now as the fireman observed, ''*Somebody* had it in for you. That window upstairs was busted from the outside. A body can tell after he's trained with our volunteer brigade a spell. The cuss who wound up out front and lobbed a Greek fire grenade through a second-story window must *not* have thought your back was turned. He must have thought you were *in* that bed at the time!''

Longarm started to ask how they could be certain it had been a *he*. But as soon as you studied on it, the bomb thrower would have had to have a good pitching arm, and Longarm had been in another bed with the only gal in town he knew that well. He nodded soberly and said, ''My door was locked from the outside with the key left in. The rascal must have done that before he went around to wake me up with a grenade through that window. Had I been in there I'd have had one hell of a time getting out with my own key in my hand and no place to put it!''

They were met out front by the local fire chief, a squad of his followers, and the usual crowd that gathered at any fire, night or day. The chief didn't argue about who Longarm was. Word gets around quickly in a small town. As they shook hands and compared notes on the little either of them knew, Longarm spotted the room clerk talking to another fireman. He excused himself from the chief and moved over to join them. He had no call to argue when the chief tagged along.

Nodding to the room clerk, Longarm said, ''I never did it. But you can bill my office for that mattress and I won't argue. I hired the room and I should have been watching closer. My boss *told* me I was heading up this way after a known killer. Now I want you to answer me true about one thing.''

The clerk said he'd try. So Longarm explained. ''I had the key you gave me in my pants when I went down the hall to wash up. Somebody put another key in my lock from outside that fit. Your turn.''

The clerk shook his head and said, ''I never gave anyone a key to your room. I never gave any sort of key to anyone this

54

evening but you and that . . . other guest. Business is slow this time of the week.''

Longarm reached in his pants for his own key to his room as he said, ''Let's try her this way then. Any hotel loses lots of keys over the years. Guests leave without remembering to turn keys in at the desk. Petty thieves stay at a good hotel for one night, keep the key, and come back a month or so later to let themselves in to their old room to steal new goodies.''

He held the key from his pocket up to the tricky street lighting as he examined it and decided, ''On the other hand, there's cheap locks, no offense, and a serious schoolmarm with a hairpin could doubtless worm open any lock this simple key goes with. I won't tell nobody if you'd like to tell me whether I'm getting warm or not.''

The clerk smiled sheepishly and said, ''There have been occasions when we couldn't find a room key and discovered another key to another room would do as well. But I'm sure there must be at least three or four basic designs to our locks upstairs. You can't just open any old door with any old key.''

The fire chief asked Longarm how any of this discussion was likely to help with his arson investigation.

Longarm said, ''You call what I'm doing the process of elimination. When you look at everything at once you can miss the buck elk staring back from the woods at you. But as soon as you eliminate leaves and twigs that you ain't after . . .''

''What have we eliminated then?'' the fire chief demanded.

Longarm shrugged and said, ''I know one or two who couldn't have done it. After that, I've barely started to clear away the brush. I don't think tracking that extra key in the door upstairs would be worth the effort. Too many ways too many folks could pick up such a common bit of hardware. Greek fire is less common. But it's made from stuff anyone could buy separately in more than one place, and put together in private.''

The room clerk asked, ''Wouldn't such a fiendish firebug

have to have studied chemistry somewhere?''

Longarm sighed. ''Nope. He'd only have to know how to read. My own education was cut short by the war. But I can mix you all the gunpowder you need from ground charcoal, saltpeter, and sulfur. Toward the end of the Cheyenne troubles the Cheyenne were starting to hammer copper bullets from telegraph wire and reload spent cartridges with homemade gunpowder and match-head primers. Stuff like that is in one fool book or another, if even a half-educated Indian bothers to look it up.''

The fire chief looked discouraged and muttered, ''Shit, that means most anybody who wants to heave fire-bombs through windows could do so if they bothered to bone up on the subject at the free library!''

Longarm nodded. ''This jasper's obvious distaste for lawmen might mean something. That fire-bomb wasn't aimed at just anybody.''

For an instant Longarm thought someone had thrown another one as the street lit up and he grabbed for his gun. Then he saw the box camera staring at him from its tripod, and realized somebody had just taken his picture with flash powder.

The fire chief beamed and answered his unspoken question with: ''*Saddle Rock Advertiser*. They've just started printing photographs of important events in these parts with a new invention. Ain't that a bitch?''

The young squirt with the camera called out, ''Mayor Givens, how's about you move over between the chief and that famous lawman from down Denver way?''

So a portly gray-haired gent Longarm hadn't been paying attention to broke ponderously from the crowd along the walk to join them with a patronizing smile. As the chief introduced them, Longarm shook hands with the big frog of their bitty puddle. But he wasn't sure he liked him.

The newspaper photographer detonated his overhead magnesium powder again as the mayor was shaking hands. Mayor Givens said, "I've been meaning to buy you a drink in any case, Deputy Long. What was this I just this evening heard about my new constable and you shooting it out with a spook up on Signal Rise?"

Longarm tersely replied, "We're still working on it, Mister Mayor. Nat Hayward would know more than me about just what happened. I was looking the other way when he got hit. Everyone who saw it seems to be convinced the shots were fired from inside a mausoleum we were just opening up."

The mayor frowned uncertainly and said, "I take it you are not convinced?"

To which Longarm could only honestly reply, "I just said I wasn't looking. I don't know for certain where the shot that put Nat on the ground might have come from. There was gunsmoke in the doorway of the mausoleum. But the place wasn't occupied by a living soul. It was small and bare. We found no secret panels. That's why we're still working on it."

As if to back his word, Sid Marner and his junior deputy, Ike, came in to join them. Marner said, "Nat sent us to find out what all the fuss was about over this way. He tried to get up and come his ownself, but the ladies wouldn't let him. You had a fire or something here?"

Longarm said, "We did. Someone set my bed on fire. Deliberate. I don't know who it was. I suspect he's somewhere in this crowd, sore as hell to see me talking to you like this. But he's still way ahead of me. He could piss on my boots and I'd never be able to accuse him of arson."

Everyone there agreed the identity of the firebug was a poser, and after a time, seeing the fire was out and it wasn't getting any earlier, the party commenced to break up.

Longarm agreed to call on the mayor the next day, and ambled back inside the hotel, where he found the room clerk talking to a man in big overalls about the mess upstairs.

Longarm announced he was in the market for a fresh key to another room. The hotel clerk said the one he had would likely let him into Room 204. So Longarm asked them not to tell anyone who asked where to find him, and carried his smoke-stained duds and saddlebags back upstairs.

He didn't go anywhere near Room 204. He found the door to Edwina's 209 unlocked. When he ducked inside, he saw she'd left her key on the pillow of the unmade bed for the maid to find in the morning. Longarm had figured such a frisky little thing might have had earlier hotel adventures. So he used her key to lock the door on the inside before he undressed and flopped back on the bed he'd been having so much fun in when that spoilsport had tried to burn them out.

The rumpled sheets still smelled of Edwina's lilac water and clean sweat. But he was a mite tired, and too satisfied, to get hard enough to stay awake. So he went to sleep, and caught better than six hours before cocks' crow. Then he got up, enjoyed a shave and whore bath in the shivery morning air, and went downstairs to see if that cow camp cook was still talking to him.

He found Edwina and all her hands had already saddled up and ridden out, as if she'd gotten them up a tad early. He was neither surprised nor too upset. He'd been wondering how you said good morning to a gal you'd been dog-styling without giving the game away.

Chapter 7

Longarm figured the soot he couldn't beat loose wouldn't hurt his already battered, dark brown Stetson all that much. One of the hostlers at the livery said he could clean those saddlebags good as ever with vinegar and saddle soap. So Longarm left his coat and vest at the cleaner's down the way, and headed over to the schoolhouse with his growing collection of photograph prints in one hip pocket.

The schoolmarm, a perky little gal who didn't look a whole lot older than the bigger kids in her mixed-grade class, had barely started an arithmetic lesson when Longarm darkened her doorway with his badge pinned to his shirtfront, earning the everlasting gratitude of the class dunce and doubtless some few others when she put a prissy fourteen-year-old gal in charge and stepped out on the front steps with Longarm. She said she was Miss Iris Jane Tyler, and asked what possible business the federal government had with her.

Longarm got out his sheaf of black and white prints, found the one he was looking for, and explained. "They tell me you took this picture of this homely mutt in the shabby dark suit and sort of Spanish hat, Miss Iris. For openers, I was wondering if that suit and hat could have been just plain black or some other dark color. I mean, my own hat and these pants would photograph black, but you can see they ain't.''

She nodded wearily, but said, ''I've had this very conversation a time or more before. They say I somehow managed to take a picture of the villain who shot Constable Crabtree. I've even been told I took a photograph of a dead man's ghost. But I just can't say if I saw anyone standing there when I was trying to get the children to stand still. I know there were others on the street as I was standing right over there, just beyond that hitching post, with my hired camera. I remember some rude folks walking between me and my pupils at the time, while others were considerate enough to hold still or walk around behind me. That dark man to one side of our group photo was obviously behaving politely. But that's all I can tell you about him. I simply wasn't aware of him, if he was there at all.''

Longarm put the prints away and got out his notebook and pencil stub as he asked if she recalled the time of day. She nodded and said it had been just after three in the afternoon, after school, with the sun behind her and the kids facing into it.

He nodded and said, ''I noticed the fine lighting, ma'am. I figured you knew something about taking pictures with a camera. You say it was a *hired* camera, not your very own?''

She nodded. ''I do enjoy taking pictures and I've my own modest kit. But in order to take that class photograph at any reasonable range, I used a professional portrait camera from Gordon's Gallery up the street. Otherwise, I'd have had to stand clear across the street to get all of my pupils on the same plate, and even then, they'd have been out of focus as well as tiny.''

Longarm nodded. ''I follow your drift. And you've already told me two more things than I knew when I woke up this morning, Miss Iris. Nobody else made note of the time, and would it be safe to assume a lady hiring a camera would get her photographic plates from the same place?''

60

She replied, "Of course. That nice immigrant lady who works there gave me more than I needed in case I did something wrong. You see, when you duck your head under the cloth behind a portrait camera, you see everything upside down on the ground-glass screen. So you have to figure out what you're doing before you slide the plate holder in and can't see anything until—"

"I know how you take a photograph," Longarm told her. "I see how easy it would be to miss someone off to one side as you were lining up to shoot. Is it possible that jasper in the dark suit came along and stopped just to one side as you were uncapping the lens, shoving in the plate holder, extracting the plate cover, and such?"

She nodded soberly. "I said as much to those other lawmen who asked about that mysterious stranger, Deputy Long. I have no memory of him standing there as I was photographing my pupils, and no, before you ask, none of the children remember anyone standing there either. Deputy Hayward took written statements from them all a few days ago and disrupted our whole morning session!"

Longarm smiled thinly and said, "In that case I won't disrupt yet another, Miss Iris. I just have one more question. You said before you had some doubt about him being there at all. Could I pin you down just a tad tighter on that? You ain't the first in town to suggest we may be dealing with something impossible, no offense."

She said, "None taken. I never said I believe in ghosts, and I'd as soon be called Iris Jane, not plain Iris, if you don't mind."

He smiled fondly and said, "In that case you can call me Custis, Miss Iris Jane. I'm glad neither one of us believes in ghosts you can capture on a photograph plate in broad daylight without cheating."

She frowned up at him defensively and demanded to know who he was accusing of what.

It wouldn't have been polite to tell a young gal not to get her bowels in an uproar. So all he said was: "I ain't sure anyone's been trying to fool the camera's eye, Miss Iris Jane. I'd be mighty surprised to discover trick photography was one of your other hobbies. On the face of it, you took an honest and upright photograph of an outlaw shotgunned, autopsied, and embalmed close to three years ago."

She gulped and replied, "Deputy Hayward showed me those dreadful prints of that dead outlaw. I agree the picture I took right here in front of my school shows the same homely features. But I don't see how they could have both been the same person! What about a mask?"

Longarm shook his head and said, "Thought of that right off. Down Denver way I once fooled a suspect myself with a waxy death mask of a murder victim. But that was in tricky lamplight at some distance. A cuss traipsing around with a false face in bright sunlight in front a classroom of naturally curious kids would have been taking a chance nobody but a total loon would have taken. On top of that, the picture he posed for on another occasion, with others crowded tight around him, shows him with a different expression."

She nodded. "Then we have to be talking about a man who simply looks a lot like that dead outlaw."

Longarm grimaced and replied, "A man who *acts* a lot like the late Deathless Dan as well. Deathless Dan Marlow had no twin brother, nor even a plain old brother. We thought of that before I was sent up here to compare notes with your town law. So we've got somebody else who's not only a total double in appearance but just as ornery, or somebody just as ornery is trying to make us *think* we're tracking a rascal who died years ago!"

She said she had no idea what he was talking about. He said

that made two of them, and ticked his hat brim to her, adding he'd wasted enough of her schoolday. She smiled archly back at him and said it had been a pleasure talking to him, and then, before he could get away, she made him promise he'd come by and tell her if he found out any more.

He didn't think he would. She was almost pretty, not too skinny, and any gal who didn't want to be messed with had no beeswax flirting with a gent. But the farther he got from the schoolhouse the less tempted he felt to go back and give her a good lesson. For she was only halfway to lovely and seemed awfully young. Grown-up gals who sent such smoke signals with their eyes tended to know how to take care of the possible consequences. It was the silly younger gals who'd been reading romantic novels instead of Miss Virginia Woodhull's tracts on free love and the woman's vote who got a man in trouble with their dear old daddies' shotguns.

He'd forgotten the schoolmarm's willowy walk by the time he got to Gordon's Gallery. A bell above the door announced him as he stepped inside, and a middle-aged galoot with fancy sleeve garters and rubber apron came out from the back, spied the badge Longarm had pinned on for the occasion, and held out a friendly hand, saying, "We've been expecting you ever since we started developing those strange plates. Hold on and I'll fetch my assistant, Valya. She's the one who does most of my darkroom work."

He went in back for a few minutes, and returned alone to say, "I called through the door to her. It shouldn't be long. But you can't open the door when she's developing plates. You see, if any other light hits the silver iodide before it's been fixed, or frozen in hypo—"

"I know how you develop those glass plates covered with goo," Longarm told him. "You'd know most of the important answers anyway, Mister . . . Gordon?"

"Phil Gordon is the name. Taking pictures is my game,"

the photographer replied, as if he said that a lot. "Don't let this getup fool you. I'm an artist with the box and a splasher with the chemicals. That's why I hired an expert, taught by a court photographer to the Czar. Or so she says. All I know about Valya is that she never, ever spoils a plate. You have no idea how easy that can be, or how hard it is to get good help out our way!"

Longarm said, "I wanted either one of you to tell me how you found those old negatives taken by the Demille sisters."

Phil Gordon blinked uncertainly and replied, "They were just *there*. I bought this place, lock, stock, and cobwebs, from the Demilles a good six months ago."

"That ain't what I asked," Longarm said. "Whenever you took over, those three-year-old negatives would have been filed away with reversed images of folks you didn't know. Yet as soon as you or your assistant developed more recent pictures of someone who was a total stranger to the both of you . . ."

Gordon laughed easily. "You're sniffing the wrong asshole, no offense. I didn't *know* what we had in the backlog of old plates until they asked us to look. It was right after somebody shot the town constable a short while ago. Witnesses had described a dark individual with a parrot nose and eyebrows that met in the middle. I would be the first to agree with you that I'd never seen anyone like that here in Saddle Rock. It was obvious he'd never come in here to have his portrait taken. Then somebody recalled that dead outlaw we *should* have had old plates on. We pulled them to make new prints to show around town. It was Valya, who'd just developed those later photographs, who noticed the resemblance and called them to our attention."

As if she'd heard her name, a smoldering brunette with Tartar eyes came to join them, wearing a chemical-stained smock over a well-developed chest. She didn't look as if she wanted to shake hands, so Longarm didn't try as Gordon introduced

64

her as Miss Valya Mirov. Longarm didn't ask her if she'd ever taken pictures of the Czar. He told her he'd just come from talking with Miss Iris Jane Tyler, and repeated what the school-marm had said about the professional camera and sealed photographic plates. The Russian gal stared across the counter like she couldn't understand a word he was saying as he went on. "You folks would likely know more than me about those photographs taken at spirit-rapping sessions. You know, the ones where the face of some dead relation seems to sort of float behind the portrait of a paying customer?"

The Russian gal just glowered.

Phil Gordon nodded and said, "Double exposure. Childishly simple parlor magic. The spiritualists illuminate a picture of some dear departed in a darkroom and take a quick shot of it. They remove and reseal the plate undeveloped until the sucker arrives. Then they pose the poor goose to take a second picture with the same plate, run the whole shebang through the dark-room, and *voila*, there's poor old Aunt Ida, smiling fondly out of the shadows from spirit world at her favorite niece."

His smoldering assistant murmured, "Is not right to tell ghost stories with camera. In my country they tell tales of very bad things that can happen to peoples who trifle with such things. I want that man in picture by school and in taproom to be just man, not *dvorovoi*."

Longarm agreed both sorts of Russian haunts sounded mean, and went on. "I ain't accusing anyone of double-exposing on *purpose*. But you did have all those ancient negatives, and ain't it a fact you make fresh plates by recoating old sheets of glass you have no further use for?"

Valya snapped, "You accuse me of being big slob who makes fresh plate with old image still there?"

To which Longarm could only reply, "Well, that thought had crossed my mind, Miss Valya."

She said something that sounded just awful in Russian. Then

she insisted in English, "You come with me, fool, and see for self what a slob Valantina Alexandrovna Mirov is, big slob!"

So Longarm walked around one end of the counter to join her as Phil Gordon laughed and said, "Enter her darkroom at your own peril, pilgrim. I'd as soon stay out here and take care of anyone who comes in while she's fooling with dangerous chemicals in the dark!"

Longarm didn't ask which might be the most dangerous. He already knew they used cyanide and Lord only knows what else to capture and freeze light on glass and coated paper.

As he followed the shorter, well-rounded Valya into their darkroom, he was mildly bemused when she threw a switch near the door to wink on an electrified ruby Edison bulb. He asked about it, and she started to explain how dim red light wouldn't expose the photographic chemicals before they were developed and fixed.

He said, "I knew that part, Miss Valya. I was wondering where you got your electric current. The Cheyenne Social Club has its own steam dynamo, but—"

"Batteries," she snapped, pointing at the duckboards under them. "In basement. Banks of wet cells to power all lights in here. Watch this."

She flipped another switch and they were flooded by the dazzle of twenty-watt bulbs set in the ceiling. Young Tom Edison's new lamps took some getting used to if you'd grown up with coal-oil light. Valya switched them off again to glower at him in the ruby glow that was left as she said, "Wastes battery acid when you use for routine work. Is nothing developing in wet-sink. Let me show you with tray of hot water how we make fresh plates."

He saw they had hot boiler water as well—another modern notion—when she turned a tap to run the water into an enameled tray. As she dropped what seemed to be exposed negatives into it Valya explained, "Negatives left over from family

66

portrait. We only file ones approved to make prints. Watch how I soak a few minutes in hot water. Glass is only backing for gelatin sensitized to light with silver iodide. In little while I strip old negative image off glass with spatula. Wash down pipe to cesspool. Nothing left but simple square of clean glass, *da*?''

He nodded. ''If you say so. I suppose there's no chance a sort of after-image could cling to the glass?''

She looked as if she was fixing to rub his nose in her tray as she snapped, ''Idiot! Image is on gelatin. Not glass. Could see, could *feel* if any of old negative was still there. Besides, pictures of *dvorovoi* on other negatives I can show you not double exposure. Were taken of somebody or something *there*!''

He asked how she knew. She ran more hot water as she called him a total asshole, or something worse, in her own lingo. Then she moved over to a chest of drawers and got something out before she winked on the bright overhead bulbs again, saying, ''Is lucky so many of you keep ordering more prints. I have negative plates ready in here. You know how to view negatives? Or do I have to run more prints for big dumb ox?''

He said, ''I reckon reading a negative is something like reading set-up newspaper type. You just have to run things through your brain sort of backwards. But what am I supposed to be looking for?''

She handed him the glass negative for the print in his pocket of the schoolchildren and schoolhouse as she answered, ''Two things. White outlines to begin with. Matching shadows after that. When faker cuts out photograph and pastes on other to reshoot, he darkens white paper edges with India ink. This shows *white* outline in *negative*. You will see none there.''

Longarm held the glass plate against the overhead lighting, and had to agree the cuss standing near those schoolkids didn't seem to have been cut out and pasted anywhere.

Valya insisted, "Look at shadows. Shadow of his hat brim and buttons on his coat. Shadow of grips of guns sticking out from under coat. Now look at same kinds of shadows on children and tell me sun was not at same angle, casting same shadows."

He couldn't. He handed back the glass plate, saying, "Miss Iris Jane says she only took that picture earlier this year. You've just told me she took a real picture of a real somebody, or something, around three in the afternoon of a bright June day. What's the difference between this here *dvorovoi* and the lichee nut you thought even less of?"

She smiled for the first time—it was a hell of an improvement—and said, "*Dvorovoi* is spirit peasants see out in yard late at night. Nobody is sure why. They only stand there, in shadows of barn or over behind woodpile. *Lichy* is met on roads through forest. Wolves are a lot safer to meet in forest. Wolves do not have *lichy*'s powers."

Then she brightened and decided, "Worse than *lichy* would be to meet *rusalka*! But *rusalka* is always girl. Woman, anyway. Some who say they have seen *rusalka* describe as beautiful girl. Others describe as ugly old hag. Not many have met *rusalka* in willows along river and come back to describe *anything*."

Longarm cocked a brow. "I've never quite been able to buy the *wendigo* some Indians worry about meeting up with in the woods. But I met one one time, and he turned out to be a big old fake."

Valya smiled uncertainly up at him and asked, "You think these are pictures of fake *dvorovoi* then?"

To which he could only reply, "They have to be. The other answer's too awful to contemplate!"

Chapter 8

It seldom snowed at that altitude that early in the fall in Colorado. But there was a taste of snow in the afternoon air, and he was just as glad to get his frock coat and vest back before suppertime. Saddle Rock was too small a town to make canvassing it on horseback practical. But it had been big enough to keep a lawman warm in his shirtsleeves as he strode from door to door.

He supped on mashed spuds and steak smothered in chili beans at a hash house near the railroad stop. He polished that off with two slices of pie, elderberry and pumpkin, because they both looked as good, had an extra cup of black coffee, and ambled on over to the Western Union office to wire a progress report to Denver.

He found a message from Billy Vail waiting for him. His boss said he'd only been sent to see if their file photographs matched the new ones shot up yonder. The prints mailed by the town law had arrived, and now Henry was bitching about Longarm having that first set. So now they wanted Longarm to bring them on back and let Saddle Rock or the Colorado State Police worry about who'd shot Constable Crabtree. For whether Longarm stayed there or not, the federal want stated Deathless

Dan Marlow had been tucked away in his coffin as far as any federal warrants read. The shooting of a local lawman by a person or persons unknown was a local matter. Marshal William Vail just didn't buy the late Deathless Dan as the killer of anyone.

Longarm couldn't argue with such simple logic. But he knew he'd never rest easy until he figured this poser out. So he ambled on up to Gordon's Photographic Gallery to see if they could run him off some duplicates of his fool prints to put on the night train for Henry to fuss over.

He saw they were still open. But when he dingled his way in, Phil Gordon came out from the back to hear him out, then said, "I'm afraid I just let Valya go home for her supper. She boards over by the schoolhouse with other spinster gals and a landlady who serves at six o'clock sharp. But there's an easier way to do it."

Longarm allowed he was game for anything that didn't hurt.

The proprietor suggested, "Why not just send those old sepia-tones you've been packing along with the black and whites we ran off for you? Those are the pictures your boss seems to want, and Valya can run off all the fresh prints you'll ever need from our filed negatives as soon as she comes in tomorrow morning."

Longarm tried to come up with a logical objection, couldn't do so, and asked if he could have an envelope big enough for the chore.

Goron gave him one, and let him use a pen and real ink to address the sealed envelope to his home office. Then Longarm hurried back to the rail terminal, scouted up the dispatcher, and explained the favor he needed.

The railroad man said they'd be proud to see the packet of prints was hand-delivered to the Denver Federal Building before dawn, which was more than any U.S. mails could say.

As they shook on it, the railroad man tossed in a remark

about Constable Crabtree having been a pal of his.

Longarm asked if he'd witnessed the killing, since Crabtree had been gunned on the station platform.

The stationmaster shook his head and said, "Not exactly. He may have been headed over this way. But he was shot down in that street yonder. That's all I can tell you about the shooting. I was down by the water tower jawing with some of the yard crew at the time. Heard gunshots and ran up this way to see what was up. By that time Crabtree was down, with a crowd already gathering around. I don't know who said he'd been having a fuss with someone on railroad property when it turned into a shootout. But that's the way it read in the *Advertiser* and the *Rocky Mountain News.*"

Longarm smiled thinly and said, "Reporters likely talked to some of the same folks I did this afternoon. You get used to that on my job. Canvassing witnesses can get a lot like talking to the bunch of blind men who'd gone to see the elephant. One grabbed the trunk, another an ear, another the tail, and so on, to leave convinced and elephant was like a python snake, an India rubber tree, a tall cow, and so on. I'm still trying to find out whether anyone described the killer as someone who looked like some photographs, or decided exactly what he looked like after they'd been shown the photographs. I got to go ask some of your less experienced lawmen about that now."

They shook on that, and Longarm trudged up to the more residential part of town with a clearer conscience but a puzzled mind. It was far easier to say the suddenly promoted and doubt-less rattled Nat Hayward had been conducting a slipshod in-vestigation than it was to say what the kid had been doing wrong. A small-town law force could only look under so many wet rocks and question so many town drunks. So Longarm wasn't really certain who was remembering what with any ac-curacy, and after a whole day of retracing Nat Hayward's ear-lier steps he hadn't come up with any new answers or, hell, thought up many new questions!

When he got to Doc Kruger's dispensary, he stepped inside and took the lemonade the doc's wife offered, even though he quickly realized he'd barked up another wrong tree. Doc Kruger came out from his examination room, after lancing a boil on a cowhand's rump, to explain how he'd sent the hip-shot Hayward home for supper. The doc said, "Both Nat and his pretty young wife were missing their feather bed, albeit I warned him, not her, to go easy with that stuff for now. His flesh wound's coming along nicely, with no fever or mortification. Barring any turn for the worse, he ought to be back on his feet by the end of the week."

Longarm asked how their new constable had made it home to supper if he couldn't walk yet.

Kruger said, "Buckboard, of course. But in point of fact, Nat walked out to the drive on his own feet, however slow. You both have to understand it's not *what* you can do but what you *ought* to be doing as you recover from a gunshot wound. It's true Nat got off lucky with no major nerves or blood vessels severed. But both flesh and bone took a nasty drilling with hot spinning lead, and I shouldn't have to tell a man with your experience how many gunshot victims die days or even weeks after they've apparently survived their wounds. What did you want with Nat anyway? I can give you his address if you need it."

Longarm said, "I don't need it. I have it in my notebook already. That's one of the reasons I take notes. Saves asking the same questions over and over. I was fixing to see if Nat could help me clear up a few conflicting details I took down this afternoon. There's nothing all that astounding. The only actual lawman who could tell us exactly what Constable Crabtree was up to when he was gunned down amid total confusion would be the late Constable Crabtree in the dead flesh, and I still doubt dead men can tell tales or pose for photographs."

Doc Kruger rolled his eyes at the ceiling and sighed. "You're really not going to ask me for another exhumation order, are you?"

Longarm smiled thinly and replied, "Not before somebody takes a photograph of *him* wandering about in broad daylight. I got enough on my plate with one missing cadaver. For even if I could figure out how someone did that, I'd still be stuck with the infernal *motive* for all this bullshit!"

The deputy coroner and local M.D. asked if lunatics had to have rational motives to rob graves and shoot at lawmen.

Longarm grimaced and said, "Lunatics may not have *rational* cause for carrying on so crazy. But they *think* they know what they are up to. A maniac who's convinced he's Jesus Christ or Napoleon still aims to save the world, on conquer it."

Doc Kruger asked, "What if someone thinks he's Robin Hood, out to rid the people of all you dreadful Norman lawmen?"

Longarm shrugged. "I read that book. It's full of bull. The English longbow was invented way after the Norman Conquest, which was one reason the Normans won. And Robin Hood, Little John, Maid Marian, Friar Tuck, and Will Scarlet all have Anglo-Norman names. You can look it up. Sir Walter Scott, being a Scotchman, must not have known real Saxons had names like Alfred, Ethelred, and so on."

Doc Kruger laughed and said, "Deathless Dan Marlow is supposed to be a Scotchman too?"

Longarm grinned sheepishly and replied, "Marlow ain't a Scotch name. I don't believe in haunts by any name. My original point was that somebody *alive* has been busting a gut to make us think we're up against a cuss I shot dead and you cut open on these very premises way the hell before somebody *else*—no, not Deathless Dan—shot poor old Constable Crabtree and faded away in the crowded, dusty confusion. I haven't been able to find half the witnesses on Nat's original list. None of

73

them I could find could give me a good description of the killer. They agreed he looked something like the mysterious stranger in those recent photographs. They also agree, if you press 'em to really think back, that they decided what the son of a bitch looked like *after* they were shown those pictures of him. Not *before*. So who could have told Nat and the others they had to catch up with that mysterious stranger to begin with?''

Doc Kruger shrugged and said, ''Don't look at me. I think Nat said some cowhand recalled the killer as a stranger he'd seen in Madame Laverne's taproom. You'll have to ask Nat who remembered that magazine photographer and the possibility we had an actual photograph to start from. As you just pointed out, things were awfully confounded around here right after we lost our town law, speaking of motives. What if the killer was out to leave us without any lawmen long enough to . . . do what?''

Longarm shook his head and said, ''It's been tried in other parts. It ain't practical. The community can appoint or send away for lawmen about as fast as anyone can gun them without getting shot himself.''

He sighed and added, ''Before you suggest a really wild shootist might not see that, I still fail to see why he shot the first one—Constable Crabtree. Have you been missing any cows? Has your one bank been robbed? Has anyone tried to stop that spur train coming or going to Fort Collins?''

Doc Kruger shook his head and said everything had been peaceful as ever in town—save for somebody gunning lawmen, that is.

Then Ike Baker tore in to declare someone had just shot the printer and busted up the press room of the *Saddle Rock Advertiser* something dreadful.

Kruger naturally tagged along in his capacity as deputy coroner. The doc could walk as fast as the two lawmen. But it was over

74

three city blocks away. So by the time the three of them got there, the premises of the shot-up *Saddle Rock Advertiser* were crowded with well-wishers or curiosity-seekers from the closer saloons and tobacoo shops along the one serious street in town.

Nat Hayward and his other deputy, Sid Marner, were starting to get more control of the press room as Longarm and Kruger arrived along with young Ike. Nat shouted through the din for Ike to pitch in and help herd everyone who had no business there somewhere else. Longarm helped some by shoving one drunk on his ass when a more polite request to let him and the doc through was ignored.

As they joined Nat Hayward and some others around a body on the floor between the type racks and the flatbed press, Doc Kruger asked Nat what in thunder he was doing on his feet after taking a .45 round in the hip so recently. The young lawman shrugged and said, "I had to take charge here. Or at least I had to *try* and take charge. I can't seem to make half these assholes listen to me."

Longarm suggested, "Deputize three or four of the bigger and more ornery assholes. I nipped a lynching in the bud one night that way."

So Nat got to it as Longarm turned to the more responsible-looking gents that Nat hadn't chased away from the body and mildly asked if any of them had any idea what had happened.

Nobody there could tell him the whole story. But as things turned out, one of them was the actual printer and owner of the paper, a sort of balding little waif of about forty called Hamish Taggert. The blond youth on a dirty floor all spattered with spilled blood and scattered silvery type would have answered to Jack Weaver if he hadn't been so very dead. His faintly smiling face was in repose with both eyelids half shut. But his pale blue shirt was a bloody mess, and when Kruger hunkered down for a closer look he decided, "Five bullet holes spaced close to the heart. I can't give you the caliber until I autopsy this poor kid. But unofficially, it looks as if the killer emptied the wheel into him at point-blank range.''

Longarm shook his head and said, ''No closer than two yards, Doc. I ain't trying to tell you how to fill out a death certificate, but that's a fairly light shirt and you'd see more powder blackening if the killer had fired from closer than six feet.''

Doc Kruger shrugged and said, ''Damned straight shooting for such a wild fusillade. Any one of those shots would have finished this boy and . . . Say, how would poor Jack have managed to stay on his feet long enough to catch the other four rounds?''

''Murder moves in mysterious ways,'' Longarm dryly replied. ''I like to see if I can catch the murderer first. He, she, or it can usually fill in the details for you if you carry some grub and booze to the jail before the hanging.''

He questioned Hamish Taggert some more to establish the dead kid as their printer's devil, or apprentice. Taggert said he'd left young Weaver to ''put the front page to bed,'' or secure the set galley of type with wedges on a cast-iron frame so type wouldn't jar loose as they printed the paper.

Longarm glanced at the type scattered all about the half-empty frame and observed, ''Somebody sure didn't want that front page printed. I don't suppose you'd have any typed-up copy that might give us some notions along those lines?''

The printer and publisher said, ''Well, sure, we have our original copy. As you just suggested, stories and advertisements are either handwritten or typed, and then I myself stick the type right over there at that compositing table. I can tell you, loosely, what each and every line of scattered type spelled out. I can get file copies from the front office if you feel they'd help.''

Longarm said, ''Start with a bird's-eye view of what that front page might have looked like if someone hadn't just scattered it all over the floor with your poor helper.''

Taggert did his best as, with half his mind, Longarm watched Nat Hayward and those two other kids get things under better control. For as far as Taggert could recall they'd had nothing more interesting than that fire at Longarm's hotel the night before planned for the front page of the small-town newspaper. Taggert explained his paper was only published once a week. So the killing made even less sense when you considered how easy it was going to be for them to just reset the fool front page and print as many copies of it as they wanted long before Monday, when it was due.

Longarm had just said he'd best have a gander at the actual copy when there came a wail from another room and that young squirt who'd been at the fire taking pictures came out to cry, "Some son of a total bitch has smashed our Ben Day projector and gone to glory with a whole drawer of negative plates!"

Longarm legged it over that way, with Taggert on his heels. As they followed the photographer into what Longarm now recognized as another darkroom with an Edison bulb in the tin ceiling, Taggert introduced the kid as Flash Fleming, his crack photographer and engraver. Longarm was too polite to comment on an obvious family resemblance. He said he had met up with Flash the night before, having his picture taken with their mayor and police chief. Fleming seemed too upset to care.

Taggert let fly a wail about their Ben Day rig as he got a look at the ornery treatment it had received at the hands of some vandal with a club or hammer.

Benjamin Day was the son of the founder of *The New York Sun*. The Day family had sold the paper early on for a princely sum, and so Ben Day, as he was called, had been raised as a sort of prince with the time and money to eat cucumbers and invent wonders. Nothing he'd invented had made him all that much money until he'd made up for lost time in the last year or so with this simple notion that was likely to change the whole printing and publishing industry.

Ben Day couldn't have done it without young Thomas Edison's electric lamp, patented in '78. But given a bright safe light to work with, the Ben Day rig shone a beam of light through a regular negative plate and then another plate of glass etched with fine crisscross lines to bust the image up into tiny dots, set tighter where the negative let more light through and wider where there was less. The result was a reversed or positive image projected on a copper plate sensitized with photographic salts. Once you'd developed your photograph print on the copper, you could dunk it in acid to etch away the metal that wasn't protected by the dots of your image. This gave you a printing plate finer than anyone could have etched by hand expensively, the way most papers were still doing it.

Taggert was muttering something about insurance as Longarm bent to switch on the inner bulb and stare morosely through the torn bellows at the shattered glass of a photographic plate and Ben Day screen that had been clipped together above the projection lens when someone had given them a good lick.

Longarm began to idly pick out bits of glass with one hand as he gathered them in the other, asking Flash Fleming if anyone had any notion what had been on the ruined negative.

Flash nodded and said, "The last plate I pulled, of course. It was that picture I took of you, the mayor, and the fire chief last night. We were running it with the story of that hotel fire."

Longarm went on gathering the glass bits as he asked how come the picture had still been in this projector if it was supposed to be with that front-page story someone had scattered from hell to breakfast.

Hamish Taggert explained. "My orders. We'd have no need for this Ben Day machine if you could print from a damned dry-plate negative. The engraving block Flash had developed in here would be out there in the press room if someone hadn't lost it on us as they busted us all to hell. We leave the Ben Day set up till we pull some proofs, see?"

Longarm gingerly put a handful of busted glass in the side pocket of his frock coat as he soberly declared, "I doubt it was lost. I figure someone didn't want his picture in your paper."

Their photographer protested, "That don't work. I only took two flash shots. I never photographed anyone but you, the mayor, and our fire chief."

Longarm said, "You mean you didn't take pictures of anyone else on purpose. I was caught by surprise the first time you shot off all that flash powder in my fool face. Who's to say who else might have been standing just a tad further back in the crowd?"

Flash said he followed Longarm's drift as, in point of fact, they both followed him out to the press room in time to see the late Jack Weaver leaving on an improvised litter. Doc Kruger explained he'd be sending the dead boy to his place for an official autopsy and sending Nat Hayward home to bed, if he knew what was good for him.

When the gimpy young lawman protested that he had to investigate the durned killing, his doctor sternly told him he'd meant it about sending him to bed early. Kruger warned, "I know you're feeling full of beans tonight, thanks to my getting all that lead out of you in one piece a damned short time ago. But I told you then and I'm telling you now that you won't be out of the woods until the last scab comes off with no green puss."

Longarm chimed in. "Do as he says, Nat. Your deputies and me can canvass the neighborhood and take down the usual or unusual answers to the usual questions."

Nat protested, "The night train's left, but the rascal could still have ridden out on his own, and if we posse up and cut his trail before he gets too far—"

"Go home and get to bed," Longarm told him. "I generally like to know who I'm after before I try to cut his damn trail. You can't go after nobody in particular with a posse.

Grown men can look silly riding in circles like a pup after its own tail.''

Nat protested, "I know. That's why we have to figure out who we're after, damn it!''

But Longarm said soothingly, "Go home, old son. Let *me* hunt for the rat!''

Chapter 9

It was barely going on bedtime for others in and about Saddle Rock by the time Longarm and the two kid deputies concluded they'd asked everyone who mattered all the usual questions without getting any unusual answers.

Nobody could recall any strangers stranger than Longarm himself around a cow town in the middle of the week when few if any of the surrounding country folks rode in. Some of the after-supper drinkers who'd run from nearby saloons at the sounds of gunplay recalled more or less than the five shots Doc Kruger figured on. Longarm explained to the less experienced deputies that you seldom got witnesses to agree on every detail unless they were in cahoots to sell the law a lie.

He was the only one who'd grasped the significance of any gunshots at all. So, seeing they seemed eager to learn, he explained. "Nobody had time to smash things up so thoroughly *after* they gunned Jack Weaver. So try her this way. They were out to make sure that one front page would never be published as planned. They found Weaver there, and so they had to throw down on him and make him hold still whilst they did what they'd come to do. Jack Weaver was shot as they were leaving. Not before they'd wrecked that Ben Day gear and stolen the photo-engraving they never wanted printed.''

Sid Marner frowned thoughtfully and asked, ''*They?* Oh, I follow your drift. It would have been tough if not impossible for one man to cover that printer's devil and do what was done. So we're looking for two or more sons of bitches who . . . Must have been known to poor Jack Weaver!''

Longarm nodded approvingly and said, ''Only way she works unless we read all the signs wrong back yonder.''

Then he fished out three cheroots, handed two out, and struck a light as he added wryly, ''That ain't saying I've never read signs the wrong way. I might have a better notion after I find out what Weaver was killed for.''

They split up out front of the Western Union. Longarm couldn't come up with anything he wanted to wire anybody just yet. So he asked a local for directions, and headed on to that ladies' boardinghouse both Iris Jane Tyler and Valya Mirov had mentioned earlier.

He found both gals out on the veranda, along with a dozen more gals and the old prune who ran the place. They were all agog about the wild gunplay and menfolk running back and forth ever since. But of course no well-bred lady was about to traipse over to Main Street unescorted after dark.

The schoolmarm, Iris Jane, looked surprised when he just nodded to her while coming up the steps and stepped over to the immigrant gal to tick his hat brim and say, ''Evening, Miss Valya. I was wondering if you'd be able to give the law a hand, seeing you're still up and have the skills required.''

The small but voluptuous brunette looked as surprised as the gals all around them. But she nodded and allowed she was willing to give it a try, whatever it was he wanted.

He explained. ''I have a sort of jigsaw puzzle of busted glass in this one pocket. Might you have you own key to Gordon's Gallery and do you reckon your boss would mind if we used some of his chemicals and paper?''

She said she doubted that, and went inside to fetch a shawl to throw over her shoulders against the night air, or leastways against being taken for trash. It was a balmy enough night for that altitude at that time of the year.

He explained more to her as the two of them walked the short way to the photography studio. Valya said she and the other gals had been told a mite about the shooting over at the *Advertiser* by passersby. She asked who he suspected. When he said they didn't *have* any suspects, she told him a Russian joke.

She said, "One day Czar can't find his pipe. Is looking all over Winter Palace for pipe and when he can't find, is calling in head of OTLEYA III."

"Say again?" Longarm demanded with a puzzled smile.

The Russian girl with Tartar eyes said, "OTLEYA III is like your Secret Service, but worse. Pay attention if you want to get joke."

He did and she continued. "Head of OTLEYA III tells Czar they will question servants and find who stole pipe. One hour later is coming back to find Czar smoking by fireplace and tell him hall porter has confessed to stealing pipe. But Czar is taking pipe out of face with smile to say he found pipe in other pocket. So they should let hall porter go. But head of OTLEYA III says they can't do this. They have already *shot* confessed thief of Little Father's pipe."

Longarm chuckled, seeing she'd tried so hard. He didn't ask her what the point of her lame joke was. Folks from other odd lands had already assured him that, rough as the law could be in These United States, things could get rougher in the rest of this harsh world.

They got to the gallery, and she unlocked the front door so they could tinkle in. They had no electrified lamps out front. As was the case at the nearby newspaper, the modernistic darkroom gear, powered by wet-cells in the cellar, was all they felt called upon to pay for. It was said that that Edison jasper was building a steam-powered electrical generating plant in New York City. But it figured to be a spell before average folks could afford to replace their good old oil lamps out this way. So he had to grope the wall some as he followed Valya back to the darkroom. It got bright as all hell when she switched on the overhead bulbs hanging from the white tin ceiling, though. As his eyes got used to the glare, he gingerly fished the shards of broken glass from his pocket, and placed them where she pointed on a zinc work surface by the sinks.

Valya spread what seemed a windowpane of clear glass next to the negative and smeared goo from a brown bottle on it. Then she picked up a shard and said, "This looks like corner. We start with corner here and see what fits, *da*?"

Valya was good at sticking busted glass together. After she had a half-dozen shards connected to the sure corner, she said something in her own lingo and turned it the other way, adding, "Was upper right-hand corner, not bottom left. Who is fat man in funny hat on this bit?"

He said that was the volunteer fire chief. Things went faster as she got closer to the center of the shattered negative. She slipped a sheet of white paper under the new glass base so she could see better as she picked out shards with more detail. They told her where to try or not as she snapped shard after shard in place. The clear goo held them good enough. She could still move things about and had to, more than once, before she was done. Some slivers were missing, making for tricky fits. But then she had all the bigger shards Longarm had given her stuck in place and declared, "Now we put in enlarger and I make bigger nine-by-ten for you, *nyet*?"

He said that sounded swell, and watched with interest as the young but knowledgeable immigrant gal shoved two plates of glass as one into what seemed like a camera aimed straight down. As she told him to stay out of her way and turned out the overhead white light to switch on the small ruby bulb over the door, Longarm said he could see she'd done this sort of work a lot, and idly asked her what on earth she was doing out Colorado way instead of in some fancier Eastern studio where swells paid real money to have their features preserved so scientifically.

As she got out a sealed envelope and tore it open in the dim ruby light, Valya sighed and said, "You are right about me doing this a lot. In old country. Some photographs I developed for reformers Little Father and his secret police don't approve made it better for me to *leave* old country. I was in Paris for while. I loved Paris, but Czar's agents did not love me. I was in New York City for while before they caught up with me. So far, no agents of Little Father seem to know I am loving view of your Rocky Mountains so much!"

Longarm blinked and looked away as a bright white light winked on for a moment. It was out again by the time he'd figured she had to be exposing the photographic paper she'd placed in their enlarger. A body surely had to get used to lights flashing on and off in this photographing business.

He declared those other pictures she'd developed in her old country must have been mighty wondrous to get her chased this far by a Czar with no sense of humor and no guilty conscience.

Valya shrugged as she filled the two trays in one sink with some chemicals from different bottles, saying, "Czar Alexander the Second is not bad as *some* Little Fathers my poor people have been blessed with. Is system, not man, most at fault. Alexander did away with evil serfdom, about time your Lincoln let darkies go free. But one man is only one man. Can only see so much and hear so much, while other men around him make sure he only sees so much and hears so much."

Longarm nodded soberly and observed, "We used to have us this king called George. He has the same sort of slickers around him to make sure he never heard anything softer than, say, shots on Lexington Green. Do you reckon your Czar Alexander has ever seen any of those photographs you developed for your anarchist pals?''

She moved the exposed print paper to the first tray as she said, ''Don't call people you don't know anarchist. Don't be so smart about pictures of dead men, women, and children by side of road before you have seen them, *da*?''

Longarm laughed and said, ''Hold on. I never voted for your fool Czar. Other folks from your old country have told me about the powder keg his fancy crowd is sitting on like a stuck-up hen. We were jawing about troubles closer to Saddle Rock, remember?''

She did. She lifted the print from the second tray to hang it on a wire above the sinks by a spring clip. Then she gasped and decided, ''Is trick photography, *nyet*?''

He stared soberly over her shoulder at the blown-up newspaper photograph. The cracks and few missing bits were distracting. But there was no mistaking the homely face in the crowd, just behind the brighter image of Mayor Givens.

Longarm quietly said, ''I doubt that young press photographer would know how to cheat at strip poker, and I was there when he took that picture. A good spell earlier, I was there when they photographed a spitting image of that ugly cuss, lying dead on a cellar door.''

She said, ''I have read of spirit photography. I don't believe is possible.''

Longarm said, ''Neither do I. Where are all the *other* haunts if a spook haunter with a camera is allowed to photograph just one or two at a time now and then?''

She didn't seem to follow his drift. So he elaborated. ''They take pictures of old battlefields and such murderous places as that tower in London all the time. Yet none of the scores of folks who died on sites like those seem to feel like posing for their portraits. As far as that goes, there can't be all that many places in this cruel world where somebody hasn't died at some time or another over the countless years. Tales of hauntings would make more sense if they were a heap more common. Makes no sense for one old creepy soul to hang around a haunted house if all the boys killed violently at Gettysburg or even Waterloo seem content to just stay dead.''

Valya sighed and said, ''There are places in my country nobody would be able to photograph through all ghosts, if ghosts of tormented souls could be photographed. So this man who keeps showing up for lens of different cameras must be *real, nyet*?''

Longarm nodded, but said, ''Likely acting spooky on purpose, if only we could figure why. He may or may not be the cuss who gunned Constable Crabtree. It's certain he ain't doing anything more honest for a living here in Saddle Rock. There ain't that many folks in town to begin with, and nobody I've shown his earlier pictures to can recall ever seeing him around town in the flesh.''

Valya asked, ''Is not possible someone found man who looks like this dead outlaw and put him up to such spooky business?''

Longarm shrugged and replied, ''To what end? I've been asking about other skullduggery in my travels. Nobody can think of none. But let's go along with your notion of some total sneak recruiting an actor who could pass for the late Deathless Dan Harlow, given black and white photography and the uncertainty of three long winters.''

She said, ''Photographs of real outlaw are not so uncertain to *me*!''

He shook his head and insisted, ''I saw Dan Harlow in the flesh as he lay dying. I've yet to lay eyes on this phantom twin he seems to have. I'd like him better as someone who just happens to look like a two-gun man if that recent double didn't have a gun on either hip, under that frock coat, and Crabtree hadn't been shot down by a brace of six-guns firing Army .45 shorts. I mean, why go out of your way to attract attention to yourself if a simple killing is all you ever had in mind? Had they just paid some gunslick the going price for killing a local man, me and the federal government never would have had call to look into it. The county sheriff's department, or at most the state police, would have been stuck with the chore, and come to study on it—''

"Listen!" she said suddenly with a frightened stare at the door.

Longarm had heard that bell out front tinkle too. He moved over by the darkroom door and started to unbolt it as he noticed for the first time how a darkroom worker had locked them off from outside light without having to study on it.

Valya whispered, "*Nyet!* Leave locked and switch off lights. I hear somebody out there in dark!"

He whispered back, "I noticed. Get in yonder corner closer to the hall. So's you'll be out of our lines of fire. Then just hesh and let me deal with this, hear?"

As she moved to the corner and hunkered down, her Tartar eyes wide as a deer fawn's, Longarm finished unbolting the door, switched on the ruby bulb, and flicked off the brighter white one over their heads. Then he drew his .44-40 to just wait, like a tabby by a mouse hole.

Valya whispered in the dim red glow, "Why is red light on? He will know someone is in here, *nyet*?"

Longarm murmured, "Developing plates, most likely. Should it be your boss, he'll knock and make sure it's safe to open this door. If it ain't, he might not. Hold the thought. I just heard a spur rowel somewhere in the night!"

A million years went by and then, sure enough, the door crashed open. So Longarm switched on the overhead lamp and, spying a six-gun sticking out of the blackness of the corridor, fired his own at the outline of lighter darkness he could just make out. Then he switched off the light again as their night creeper fired blindly, confounded by the blinking light flashes. The man's spurred boots sounded unsteady under him as he backed off, firing wildly in Longarm's general direction as the tall deputy emptied his own wheel in reply.

Then he slammed the door, threw the bolt, and switched on the white overhead bulb to reload amid the fading fumes of gunsmoke as he sighed and muttered, "I never have that infernal Winchester handy when I seem to need it most. But I suspicion I winged him."

Being as curious as most women, Valya asked him who it had been and whether they were trapped in there or not.

He replied, "I've no idea who he was, but I'm pretty sure I know what he wanted. I doubt it was your fair white body, no offense."

As he thumbed in another round he continued. "As to our being up a tree if he's still out there, I doubt he's still out there, if he can still walk. A man would be a fool to stick his head outside just now, but all that gunplay will surely bring lots of company in the very near future."

As a matter of fact, it seemed to take less time than that before they heard a familiar voice calling, "What's going on back yonder? I smell lots of gunsmoke and Pete Calhoun says some jasper just run out of here!"

Longarm called out, "That you, Marner?" The young town deputy Sid Marner called back, "Me and half the card house. To what might we owe this disturbance of the peace just as I was holding a fair hand?"

Longarm unlocked the door to spill light out and let Sid Marner and some others crowd in before he and Valya could get them all aimed the other way.

At Longarm's suggestion, Valya lit oil lamps front and back as he filled Marner and the half-dozen late-night card players in on what little he really knew.

Pete Calhoun, a dignified drunk in a suit and startched shirt, had not been playing cards across the way when he'd heard all hell bust loose and had seen a dark figure fly out the front to ride off on a dark horse. Nobody else had even heard hoofbeats, and one unkind soul was heard to imply old Pete saw lots of things in the dark when he'd been working late with a jar of corn squeezings on his desk.

Then Sid Marner found a trail of blood spatters leading along the corridor and declared, "Whatever Pete saw, it was bleeding like a stuck pig! I got to go tell our boss, Nat Hayward. He'll surely want us to posse up and ride out after the wounded bastard!"

Longarm didn't try to stop Sid as he and some of his pals ran out the front door, whooping and yelling to others in the street. Longarm simply couldn't say whether their mysterious visitor had a nearby hideout in town or was riding the range lickety-split with at least one round of .44-40 in him.

Eating the apple one bite at a time, Longarm showed the townsmen who'd remained the latest photograph of what appeared to be a long-dead outlaw. The only one with a thing to offer was a young rider in blue denim under a Spanish hat, who allowed he *might* have seen that same face a month or more ago, though not in Saddle Rock.

When pressed to study harder by Longarm, Spanish Hat was sure it had been down at the county seat and in some shop. But he couldn't pin things down any more than that. He explained he'd only paid the least attention to the ugly mutt because the stranger had been ahead of him in the shop and he'd had to wait and stew a spell while gazing at the pest.

Longarm suggested, "Half shut your eyes and picture the whole scene in your head. See if you can remember anything else about a day you wanted something and this stranger stood betwixt you and it."

The cowhand frowned and decided, "He smelled funny."

A big gray cat got up and turned around in Longarm's belly as he quietly urged, "Funny in what way? Like something was rotting there in Denmark?"

Spanish Hat thought back, shrugged, and declared, "Just funny, like he'd been eating or smoking something I'd never smelt before. I doubt I was smelling a dead man, if that's what you're getting at. I stood no more than a yard away as he was jawing natural with the gal ahint the counter."

"A *gal* behind a counter, you say?"

It suddenly worked. Spanish Hat brightened and said, "Candy shop! I remember now, I was there to buy some violet preserves for this Fort Collins gal who fancied them. She didn't fancy me half as much, dad blast her, and this other poor cuss was searching for another gal who'd done *him* dirt. He showed a picture to the shop gal. She said his gal was Chinese."

Longarm glanced around before he saw it was safe to observe that a true-hearted woman could seldom be found. He'd noticed Valya had been sort of quiet since the shootout, and he wasn't surprised to see that the poor little thing had apparently faded away in the night. It was no skin from his nose if she aimed to make it back to her boardinghouse on her own. She'd given him all the help he'd asked for. He couldn't think of anything else she could do for him that sounded decent.

The cowhand who'd bought candy for another gal couldn't pin the shop in Fort Collins down any tighter. Longarm decided it hardly mattered this late in the game. For the shop gal serving the odd-smelling cuss had doubtless served a hundred since, and even if she remembered him, it seemed doubtful anyone would leave a name and address every time he bought a bag of candy.

The notion that a spitting image of the late Deathless Dan might be hankering for some Chinese gal didn't seem so odd when you studied on it. No matter who or what he looked like, a gent made of living flesh and blood stood to have the same needs and cravings as any other poor mortal. It seemed tough to picture Queen Victoria stuffing her royal face and taking a royal crap too. But that's what folks did, as long as they were alive.

It was sort of comforting to feel so sure that beak-nosed bushy-browed son of a bitch had to be a regular human being. Or at least a human being. He'd been carrying on too strange to be considered regular.

Chapter 10

It was pushing midnight and the dark streets were as quiet as any gaveyard as Longarm stode at last toward his new hired room at that hotel. He'd tipped the room clerk and been promised he'd be the first to know if anyone came around to ask which room he was in now.

He was walking in low-heeled boots, well-broken-in, with no spurs. But a man still clunked a mite along a wooden walk, and that somehow made the darkness all around seem even more deserted.

Then someone called his name smack behind him, and he came down in the dusty street facing back the way he'd just been, gun drawn in midair as he'd spun.

Phil Gordon, the photographer Valya worked for, stepped out from the shadows of the overhang with a derisive snort to declare, "You must really have a guilty conscience. Do I look dumb enough to yell at a man with a gun before I shoot him in the back?"

Longarm saw Gordon's hands were empty in the moonlight. So he put his own back in its cross-draw holster as he quietly observed such things happened, explaining, "Gun waddies out to make a name seem to have this here Code of the West. I never said anyone was out to backshoot me, Phil. But someone tried to front-shoot me earlier in your very own darkroom.''

Gordon said, ''Valya told me just now. Whoever gave you any right to risk her life and my property like that, you arrogant bastard?''

''Don't ever call me a bastard again with both hands empty,'' the lawman answered ominously. Then he sighed and said, ''Leaving the virtue of my parents out of it, you're right about the other two mistakes I made and I'm sorry. I was able to scout up your assistant easier because she'd told me where she lived. I asked her if she had to have your permission. She didn't know you were likely to act this hard-ass about it. I wasn't expecting anyone to trail us to your shut-down gallery. That ain't offered as a valid excuse. It was a pure mistake and I just said I was sorry. But nobody on our side got hurt, and the busted photograph negative Valya was able to save for evidence was interesting as hell. Didn't she tell you that?''

Gordon nodded grimly. ''She did. Did she tell you she was spoken for?''

So there it was, out in the open, like spit on the tablecloth.

Longarm calmly replied, ''I never asked. I wasn't sparking your true love, old son. I was asking a professional photographer to develop a damned negative for me. She did. That's all she did. That's all I ever asked her to do. So why are we talking like schoolboys about a woman who's worked in Paris and New York City, for Gawd's sake?''

Gordon said, ''I want your word you'll stay away from her from now on. I mean that.''

To which Longarm could only reply with a thin smile, ''I'm making you a counter-offer. I have no intention of riding off into the cool shades of evening with anyone employed by yourself unless I'm invited. If I want to question either of you again in my official capacity, I will. If you ever come at me so threatening again, I mean to put you on the ground, with my fists or my gun, depending on which seems the way you prefer. So you'd best start swinging here and now or go home and strap on a gun. I mean that. I got too much on my mind to play kid games over gals I've never messed with, you lovesick asshole!"

From the way Gordon sucked in his breath it seemed clear he wasn't used to being spoken to so plainly. Longarm turned away to stride on, disgusted with himself as well. For he'd never liked bullies, and even when he had to bully one back it left a bad taste in his mouth. Gordon growled good, for a man too smart to wear a gun when he got to pawing the dust over womankind. Longarm doubted he'd really gotten Valya to agree she was his true love. She was still boarding with all those other young spinster gals, and he knew that if *he'd* ever swapped spit with such a smoldering little thing and gotten her to say she was his own, she'd sure as hell be out of that boardinghouse pretty quick!

He got to his hotel and wearily turned in. He had his room key in a coat pocket. The balding night man called him to the desk anyway, softly telling him, "You have a visitor upstairs. She tipped me four bits to let her in so's she could wait for you and surprise you, she said. I thought I ought to tell you anyhow."

Longarm snapped a silver dollar on the fake marble counter to prove the older man had guessed right as he quietly asked, "You say my mystery guest is *female,* pard?"

The clerk made the cartwheel vanish as he cackled and replied, "I doubt she's a hooker. I've seen her around town from time to time and, to tell the truth, I was surprised to find her so bold!"

Longarm allowed that made two of them, and turned away to mount the stairs to the second floor. One pale night lamp was pretending to be a glowworm down the hallway. He found his door unlocked when he went to put the key in its hole. So he just stepped inside and softly said, "I just now talked to your true love about you and me, honey. To tell the pure truth, I thought he was way wrong about us."

There was no answer. As he approached the bed in the darkness he could tell by her breathing she was no longer with him. He chuckled, and declared it had been a long day for him too as he sat down on the bed beside her to shuck his boots. Although he hardly felt as ready for sleep as anyone from Russia by way of Paris. Gals had to have been around a lot if they could fall asleep that soon after so much excitement.

She stirred in her sleep as he finished undressing, hung everything up, and slid under the covers with her. As he took her in his arms he saw she'd stripped down to just her silky chemise. She felt somewhat less fleshy than she'd looked with all her duds on. But there was enough cuddly perfumed nakedness under that wispy silk to get any man stiff as a poker on short notice. So he kissed her sleepy lips and ran his free hand where it would do them both the most good as she sleepily murmured, "Ooh, Custis, what are you *doing* to poor little me?"

That didn't sound at all like Valya Mirov. But he didn't care as he replied to her dumb question by stroking her wet slit faster and harder while he tongued her back. For *who* she might be just didn't seem as important as the way she was spreading her thighs to thrust up and down with her hips as she gasped, "Don't let me waste this on your damned fingers, you sweet fool!"

So he forked himself aboard and helped her peel her chemise off over her head as she swallowed his old organ-grinder to the roots with her legs wrapped tight around his waist, sobbing, "Ooh, yess! I do like it better without a stitch of clothing in the way!"

That made two of them, although he knew for certain it was neither the earthy Edwina Chaffee nor the sultry Valya Mirov.

It would have been a tad rude to ask a lady he was coming in just who on earth she might be. So he never did until they'd both come, vowing eternal love and devotion, and it seemed safe to strike a light for a shared smoke.

Longarm managed not to gasp in surprise when he found himself in bed with the shyly smiling, totally bare-ass, and likely far-too-young schoolmarm, Iris Jane Tyler!

The innocent-looking little gal waved a pretty hand between them as he offered her a drag on his cheroot by lamplight, asking him what sort of a girl he thought she was and demanding he trim that wicked lamp and stop staring at her titties.

He left the bedlamp lit as he blew smoke the other way to assure her he wouldn't dream of tempting her with tobacco. He never said she could cover her perky breasts if she didn't want anyone admiring them. She said she tried to avoid picking up new habits because she'd found it tough to avoid the few bad habits she had.

He said he'd noticed some bad habits were tough to break. He told her what Mister Mark Twain had said about giving up tobacco. He agreed it was easy to quit cold, three times a day.

She tweaked his privates playfully under the covers and asked if he'd ever tried breaking *that* bad habit.

He chuckled, snuggled her closer with his free hand, and replied, "Not since I found out how good it felt. I'm sure glad you enjoy such hard feelings your ownself. For to tell the truth, I wasn't expecting this evening to wind up so delightful."

She pouted. "I know. I was hoping against hope you wouldn't get anywhere with that immigrant slut Valya. I saw the way you two were looking at one another back at the boardinghouse."

He had a better hold on what had possessed her to sneak into his hired bed now. Since the damage had been done, he felt it safe to blow a thoughtful smoke ring and observe, "I knew this old boy whose wife made him wear a wedding ring.

He was a whiskey drummer who spent lots of time in strange towns and so, despite that ring and some promises, he always seemed to wind up like this in some strange hotel room.''

''Are you calling me a small-town hooker?'' the bawdy little gal demanded ominously.

He patted her naked shoulder and said, ''Perish the thought. As I told you whilst we were coming just now, it's different with you and me. I was talking about this married-up whiskey drummer whose wife left him after he'd strayed once too often. He told us he was just as glad, since she'd been getting shrewish as well as hefty, whilst he was out on the road most of the time in any case. So he threw away that wedding ring and commenced to chase gals seriously.''

She began to play harder with him under the covers as she said she was glad for his whiskey-drumming pal.

Longarm chuckled and said, ''He suddenly found it easier to sell tea in China than to get strange gals, or even gals he already knew in a biblical sense. It was as if they'd all lost interest at once in such fun with strangers. But then, being a whiskey drummer and hence a keen student of salemanship, he figured out what he was doing wrong. He picked up a new ring, used, in a hockshop, put it on his finger as of old, and proceeded to make new friends everywhere he went. He said he'd found a wedding band on a man's hand had much the same effect on women as a wriggle-worm on a hook has on pan fish.''

The schoolmarm gave a dainty cough as some of his smoke drifted her way, and declared, ''I could never go out walking with a married man. What we've just done seems wicked enough, and you had no right to take advantage of me that way, you brute.''

He got rid of the cheroot and slid the hand under the covers to grab her wrist and move her hand faster as he soberly suggested she could leave if all of this seemed so brutal.

She squeezed his semi-erection more firmly as she sighed

and said she'd been praying to the Lord to give her the strength, but alas, in vain. She said, "I've never been able to stop myself, once I get sort of gushy down yonder for one of you mean things. But I never expected you to come in and just leap on me like some animal! I mean, I thought we'd talk about this and that when you came home, and then we'd get to this after, you know, a romantic interval."

He said, "You should have stayed awake. I'd have doubtless been a fool and talked your ear off whilst we were both smoldering away in our poor crotches. Lord knows, I came home with enough to talk about."

But they didn't talk about much for a spell as he kicked the covers off and forked a slender leg over each of his elbows to spread her wider and make her say "Ah!" as he probed her as deep as the two of them could manage to get him. She begged him to blow out the lamp, whimpering she wasn't used to carrying on so brazenly with no clothes on. But he told her she hadn't known what she was missing, and had her whimpering for wilder postions by lamplight in no time at all. He was too polite to ask where she'd learned some of them, with or without the lamps lit.

They wound up with her on top, reclining her bare little cupcakes agaist his naked chest as he soaked it up inside her and she said mean things about that immigrant gal again.

Cupping her bare buttock with a friendly palm, Longarm told her she wasn't being fair. By this time they were both sated enough for her to pay some attention as he explained, or tried to explain, the mysterious goings-on at the photographer's.

She said she still thought Valya was a stuck-up slut, but looking on the bright side, she purred, "Maybe now you'll believe me when I say I never faked that photograph of that spooky stranger, right?"

"It never occurred to me that you could have taken a trick photograph," he lied. "If there had been some way to doctor the undeveloped plates you turned in to Phil Gordon and Miss Valya, I fail to see how they could have faked that picture Flash Fleming took with a different camera to develop himself in his own darkroom.''

He encouraged her to move her sweet rump a mite as he added in a conversational tone that he'd about sliced her clean of suspicion with old Occam's razor.

She stiffened despite the stiffness she felt inside her, and said she didn't go in for any of that cruel stuff espoused by crazy old Frenchmen. Then, being a schoolmarm, she recalled how William of Occam had been a monk in olden times who'd gotten in trouble by teaching old-timers to think logically. She bounced just enough to tease them both as she sweetly asked what Longarm wanted to slice away from her with Occam's imaginary razor.

He said, ''I was taught the method by my boss, Marshal Billy Vail. He's a thundering wonder at whittling cases down to manageable numbers of suspects with possible motives. Brother Occam taught that whenever you had more than one logical answer, your best bet was to shave off the least possible of the two. I'd already decided a real man made up to look like a dead man had to be more possible than a dead man up and about. I had to consider flimflam photography, no offense. But I just can't see you, Flash Fleming, and Phil Gordon being in cahoots to fob fake photographs off on anyone.''

She said she didn't know that newspaper photographer, save by sight.

He said, ''That's what I mean. Could you ease forward on my dick a mite? It don't bend downwards worth mention. It would have been simple to doctor that class photograph you took, with or without your permission. It gets tougher as soon as you consider a newspaper man developing a dry plate from another camera in his own darkroom. Had anyone connected with the *Saddle Rock Advertiser* wanted us to see a fake photograph, they'd have simply published it on the front page. Had they had some call to change their minds, they'd have only had to run that story about the fire without any pictures. They had no call to kill a staff member and bust up an expensive Ben Day setup.''

She purred, ''Ooh, that feels so swell, darling. Isn't it obvious the ones who killed that poor Weaver boy were outsiders who didn't want that picture going out all over the front page of even a small-town newspaper?''

He growled, ''That's what I just said,'' as he rolled her over to brace her on her hands and knees. She gasped, ''Ooh, not with that lamp burning!'' as he rose and swung into position behind her for some good old barnyard rutting. He insisted he liked to see what he was getting into and continued. ''Me and Brother Occam seem to have *you* eliminated as a crook in cahoots with the haunt of Deathless Dan Marlow. That means I can do this to you all I want without compromising myself as the arresting officer.''

She arched her spine to take him deeper as she asked why on earth he'd want to arrest a poor gal who only wanted to have fun. He pounded on to glory as he explained, between gasps for air, how silly it felt when a defense attorney complained in front of a judge and a jury about tainted testimony.

''That's what they call it when you screw a suspect before you get the goods on her, tainted testimony,'' he said.

She allowed she'd share just a puff or two of tobacco the next time she allowed him to stop just long enough for a smoke. From the way she inhaled he wondered idly why she felt the call to giggle and complain he was teaching her all sorts of wicked habits.

So far, the only wicked habit he doubted she might have would've been called criminal conspiracy had he been suspicious she was in league with some warped mastermind, and had he had the least notion what the sneaky son or daughter of Satan behind all this had on his or her warped mind!

101

Chapter 11

The less-than-lethal schoolmarm slipped out of Longarm's bed in the wee small hours lest she miss breakfast at her boarding-house and have to explain why later to other giggling gals.

After his own breakfast of steak and potatoes, Longarm dropped by the Western Union to see if there were any answers to the few wires he'd sent out the day before.

There was one from Billy Vail. His boss wanted him to pack it up and head on home, seeing he'd never been sent north to do more than he already had. Vail agreed the purely local case seemed spooky as all get-out, but that didn't make it federal.

Longarm tore off a telegram blank to reply that someone had pegged a few shots at him the night before while he was pack-ing a federal badge in his damned pocket. He added that that seemed worth at least another day or more, knowing the week-end was coming up, and told the Western Union clerk he wanted it sent at day rates, which, like night rates after sun-down, meant the telegraph company would transmit your cheaper words in their own good time when their wires were idle. With any luck, Billy Vail would get the polite answer to his own wired orders in no more than twenty-four hours.

He ambled over to the town hall to ask who kept the vital

statistics for Saddle Rock. A shy little secretary gal led him in to see the same Peter Calhoun he'd met at the photography studio the night before. The town clerk looked more sober and less cheerful in the harsh light of day. The network of small busted veins in his sort of swollen nose said old Pete was as heavy a drinker as you usually found holding down a steady job. But he seemed to know his job when Longarm took the seat he'd been offered next to Calhoun's rolltop desk and told him what he'd come for.

Pete Calhoun nodded and said, "Some detectives from the county sheriff's department were interested in the same figures when they came up from Fort Collins right after Constable Crabtree's killing. So I can tell you without digging through the files so soon after searching them in vain. It's been peaceful to the point of yawning in these parts, save for a stolen horse here, some missing beef there, and the widely spaced shootouts between yourself and Dan Marlow, or the more recent one between poor Crabtree and a person or persons unknown. Nobody's tried to rob our one bank or stop our spur train down to Fort Collins. Things have been so slow the tinhorns and whores have been moving away."

Longarm reached for some cheroots as he frowned thoughtfully and replied, "Do tell? I had the impression someone had *run* Madame Laverne and her soiled doves out of Saddle Rock."

As he handed a smoke to the town clerk, Calhoun said, "Mayor Givens would as soon have everyone think so, seeing this is an election year and everyone's gotten so prim since Lemonade Lucy Hayes commenced to serve fruit punch at the White House, bless her pure little heart. But since you ask, and I keep such records as they pay me to keep, the old bawd and her underemployed employees moved down to the county seat because there's more, er, work down there. The cattle buyers don't bother with outlying shipping points these days."

Longarm nodded. "I noticed. A lady who gathers odd lots of beef to herd over the Divide to mining camps at more modest profit explained that part to me."

He thumbed a match-head aflame to light both their smokes as he went on. "I'll ask the killer when I catch him what Constable Crabtree and him were really fussing about if it wasn't the usual protection money. But seeing we're on the subject of whores, I was out to the cemetery the other night and nobody could explain to my satisfaction why a mausoleum purchased for the repose of wayward gals has so few customers. Herb Norman said you just hadn't had that many whores die in these parts natural or unnatural. Your turn."

Calhoun shrugged and leaned back in his chair to blow a smoke ring at the ceiling as he said, "Six, or make that no more than eight all told in the four years Madame Laverne was corrupting our youth here in in Saddle Rock. No deaths worth the time of the county grand jury, as far as Doc Kruger could tell. I have the damned death certificates in one damned drawer or another if you really need them."

Longarm said, "I hate paper dust too. So let's just go with how come Herb Norman told me different."

Calhoun shook his head and said, "Old Herb's all right. He's put more than one poor family's dearly departed in the ground for way less than it cost him to have the damned grave dug. Only two dead whores and that one dead outlaw killed in a whorehouse yard wound up in that mausoleum because that was all Madame Laverne paid for. The other half dozen or less got shipped home to their kin. It's surprising what a stern father will forgive when you wire him his wayward child has up and died before him. That glorified doghouse of scab-colored stone was never used by anyone who had a soul who gave a shit about them."

Longarm nodded as if satisfied. But he wasn't. So he asked if he could have copies of every death certificate filled out in

Saddle Rock for the past seven years, adding, "Seven years is the usual statute of limitations for anything less than murder in the first."

"But Saddle Rock wasn't *here* seven years ago," the tiny town's only recorder of vital statistics explained. "The railroad only ran this loading spur up here four years ago. The boom we all moved in to enjoy never boomed worth mention. I'll have my girl dig out the papers on everyone who's ever died around here and deliver them this afternoon. But you're likely to find them dull reading."

They shook on it, and Longarm headed for the nearby bank, the only one in town. Before he got there he met up with Deputy Constable Sid Marner, who told him he'd missed all the fun of a moonlit ride in a big tedious circle, adding, "The moon was bright and we was riding wide across overgrazed range with the ground still soft from that rain we had a week ago. Nat figures the rider who shot at you last night followed the wagon trace or railroad tracks south. No other way he could have rid without leaving sign. Nat wired Fort Collins to be on the prod for wounded riders."

"Nat Hayward was riding posse last night, with that bullet hole in him still oozing, if I know bullet holes?" Longarm asked.

Marner said, "I told him I could lead the boys faster. But old Nat can be a stubborn cuss when he thinks you're trying to boss him around. He rode, all right. We never rode hard, and he said it only hurt if he tried to stand in his stirrups at a trot. He said it didn't bother him at all if he loped his old sorrel barb. Where you headed now, Longarm?"

The federal lawman replied, "Over to your one bank. I know nobody has been making any sudden withdrawals, but it's been my experience a strange bunch in town tends to snoop around a strange bank a spell before they announce their intentions. That's how the James-Younger gang got spotted in Northfield that time. But most times, small-town folks ain't that observant, no offense."

Sid Marner didn't seem insulted, and so they parted friendly. Longarm was only mildly surprised to find Mayor Givens in the considerable flesh in a back office when he asked out front to see their bank manager.

Givens waved him to another seat across a more impressive desk as he asked whether Longarm wanted to see him in his capacity as mayor, bank manager, realtor, or insurance under-writer.

Longarm wasn't surprised to find an ambitious man with piggy eyes and so many fingers in so many small-town pies. Horace Greeley had *told* young men to go West if they aimed to die rich.

Longarm smiled thinly and replied, "I hadn't considered in-surance, Mister Mayor. But first I'd as soon make sure that misdirection this close to Halloween ain't aimed at your cash reserves."

"Misdirection?" asked the banker cum mayor uncertainly.

Longarm nodded and said, "Button, button, or which shell might the pea be under. All this bull about dead men posing for their photographs and lawmen getting shot at reads like some razzle-dazzle plot to have us all looking the wrong way when something else is pulled a tad sneakier. They gun the only really experienced lawman in these parts, and then go out of their way to have a federal deputy sent all the way from the state capital. So what happens next? They aim to soap all the windows along Main Street or tip over some shit-house?"

The fat man shrugged. "The sheriff's department and even young Nat Hayward have been over this same ground with me, Deputy Long. There simply haven't been any serious crimes up this way. That mysterious stranger who looks like a dead outlaw hasn't spoken to anyone any of the respectable folks in town might know."

Longarm nodded. "Pete Calhoun just explained why you have so few *less*-respectable folk in town these days. Let's talk about that insurance you just mentioned. You say you sell a heap of it?"

Givens shook his pudgy head and explained. "Just a sideline, mostly in connection with bank mortgages. It's a pain to have borrowers die on you. We require debt insurance on any really big loans."

Longarm wasn't certain he understood. "Let's see if I got this straight. The policies you sell name this bank as the beneficiary and only pay back money you've already loaned out?"

Given nodded primly. "That's about the size of it. Are you suggesting someone plans to insure the late Dan Marlow and then kill him for the insurance money?"

Longarm had to grin sheepishly at the picture. But then he asked if Givens knew of anyone else in town who might be worth a whole lot of insurance money to somebody less dead.

Given shook his head and firmly replied, "You're talking about a simple life insurance policy. We don't sell those. You'd have to send away for one of those mail-order, or get some insurance agent to come up this way from busier parts. A man would go broke selling nothing but life insurance policies around here."

Longarm quietly asked, "What if he didn't know that? What if a man who accidentally looked just like a dead outlaw was to poke about in these parts trying to peddle insurance or, hell, French postcards, and just had his own picture taken by accident around the time poor Constable Crabtree . . . Hold on. He was at that fire the other night as well, and I've never heard tell of a door-to-door salesman nobody in a small town could remember talking to!"

Givens said he had no idea what Longarm could be driving at.

To which Longarm could only reply, "Neither have I. Mention of insurance policies must have just turned over a wet rock in the back of my suspicious mind. Nobody seems to be heavily insured or collecting any insurance money in these parts. Pete Calhoun's fixing to send me copies of every death certificate made out in your new township, and Doc Kruger would have noticed if he'd been signing insurance forms of late. No insurance company would ever pay off a survivor without any discussion of the death with local authorities.''

He started to say something else. Then he reflected on how thick the courthouse gang in your average small town could get, and decided it might be better to question the ones who'd have the damned answers.

He trudged on to Doc Kruger's place, where he found the deputy coroner out back mulching his kitchen garden. Kruger howdied him, and explained his red cabbage had been known to last well after a white Christmas, given plenty of straw around its roots and not too much water in the dirt above the frost line.

Longarm said, "We had some winter frost when I was growing up in West-by-God-Virginia, Doc. Herb Norman was only able to explain them two dead whores in Madame Laverne's mausoleum out on Signal Rise. I just now heard from Pete Calhoun that there were others. I was hoping someone could tell me which story to buy."

Doc Kruger leaned on the handle of his rake with a smile and told him, "Nobody lied to you on purpose, Deputy Long. There were exactly eight deaths on the premises of Madame Laverne over the few years I served as her physician. Seven fallen women and one male piano player who couldn't make up his mind whether he was a drunk or an opium addict. I signed all their death certificates as attending physician and deputy coroner. I reported some few bumps and bruises to both Constable Crabtree and the sheriff's department down in Fort Collins. No charges were ever filed against anyone. Most of the deaths seemed to be the natural results of pills, liquor, and social diseases. Women can abide an incredible ammount of fornication as long as they're relaxed and willing. Some take more medication for their nerves than I would ever prescribe. But you can buy patent medicines based on both alcohol and opium or cocaine in any drugstore.

"Flypaper too," Longarm said with a grimace. "That flypaper made with honey and arsenic makes it easy to kill yourself or anyone else without going near a drugstore or a hardware that might recall the sale of rat or coyote poison. But never mind how all them whores and a professor might have died. I'd rather someone told me why your undertaker only counted two."

Doc Kruger shrugged and said, "That's easy. Madame Laverne was generous with her ill-gotten gains, but not foolish. So she felt no call to pay for the services of two undertakers for one corpse. I think Herb Norman was a little miffed at us for just packing them in pine and putting them aboard the train. I suppose he only counts the local deaths he gets a piece of."

Longarm allowed that made sense, but asked, "Who embalmed the six stiffs old Herb never counted? I know for a fact that the railroads won't let you ship unrefrigerated raw meat."

Kruger nodded. "Don't tell Herb I told you, but I could teach *you* how to drain a drawn corpse and refill the veins with his secret solution in one grim evening. I prefer the army formula for shipping bodies home by rail. Arsenic disolved in formaldehyde and alcohol. It lasts longer than that glorified strawberry syrup the professionals use, and if they turn dark along the way, so be it. A body embalmed army-style is good for six weeks aboveground, and you just never know when a freight car may be run off onto a siding in warm weather."

Longarm grimaced again. "They've been trying to outlaw arsenic embalming now that they have a test to detect flypaper dessert a good spell after the funeral. But I reckon that clears up the mystery of the nearly empty crypt. Can you tell me whether Madame Laverne was run out of town like some say, or left of her own free will?''

Doc Kruger said, ''Both. She told me when she paid for my last examination of her working girls. Mayor Givens and his party machine found her bawdy behavior a bother in an election year, while Madame Laverne and her girls found it tougher to draw a crowd no matter how they draped themselves over the windowsills when the herds were in town. We're just not getting the cattle drives we used to, now that the railroads have run so many spurs out from the older stock-shipping centers. I believe she and her girls have relocated near the stockyards in Fort Collins. Our local whoring has been taken over by an old bawd and her four daughters who ought to be ashamed of themselves. I don't attend or examine any of them. I advise young cowboys to stay the hell away from them. So far, I'm treating two who didn't for the clap.''

Longarm nodded. ''I'd heard Madame Lavern was alive and well in Fort Collins, whether she was shoved or went willing. Do you know if she's ever taken out insurance policies on any of her working crew, Doc?''

Kruger smiled incredulously and marveled, ''*Insurance?* On a posse of trail-town pussy? Surely you jest! I can't see any insurance agent offering, and if he did, I can't see any company underwriting such a policy for premiums any whorehouse could afford.''

Longarm said, ''If they did, you'd have known. Anyone who takes out a life insurance policy has to show a clean bill of health from a licensed physician and you're the only one in town.''

He got out his notebook as he quietly added, ''So how's about that?''

Kruger looked puzzled, and asked what they were talking about.

Longarm said, "Life insurance. Did Constable Crabtree have any? Has anybody died around here at a handsome profit to anyone else?"

Kruger nodded in sudden understanding and declared, "You do have a suspicious mind, don't you? I have filled out a few policy forms for a handful of folks here in Saddle Rock, now that you mention it. The poor widow of Constable Crabtree got a thousand dollars, or less than he'd have brought home as salary in two years. From the way she took his death, I suspect she'd have rather had him earn it the hard way."

Kruger thought. "Mayor Givens has a handsome policy. I hope white lies about overweight aren't federal offenses? His heart seemed sound enough for a man his age and sloth."

Longarm wrote the name down without other comments. Kruger thought and said, "I'll have to go through my files if you need a complete list."

Longarm shook his head and said, "I'm only concerned about recent payoffs on life-insurance policies."

Kruger looked relieved and declared, "That's easier. Miss Sarah Ann Breen, spinster, aged seventy-three, survived by a niece back East. I put natural causes on the death certificate. I thought it seemed only natural for a lonely old woman to drink alone like that, and the policy was only for eight hundred dollars. That's the only insured death since a railroad worker was crushed between cars before Crabtree was shot. I frankly think you're wasting your time on that suspicion."

Longarm said, "You have to eat the apple a bit at a time, and the way you whittle down your suspicions calls for slicing off one after the other until only one seems likely. Was that railroad man killed after folks started seeing that mysterious double of Deathless Dan Marlow around town?"

Kruger was commencing to sound a tad testy as he replied, "Lord, I don't know anyone who's actually seen that spooky stranger in the flesh or something odder. Hiram Greenspan was killed over in the rail yards in early March. In front of witnesses. He was coupling cars and must have stumbled, drunk or sober. They had a dreadful time getting those cars uncoupled again, once the steel knuckles had locked inside the poor boy's chest. I pronounced him dead on the spot, before they got to work with the butcher's saw. Didn't somebody tell me that teacher took the first picture of that stranger a little later in the year?''

Longarm nodded. ''He seems to have been at that fire the other night too. I can't make him fit as an insurance salesman. For which I thank you. Like I said, one bite at a time and every bite is one less to go.''

They shook on that, and Longarm trudged on to Herb Norman's combined hardware and undertaking establishment. Norman's faded but once-pretty wife said her man was out at the cemetery with his hired help.

When Longarm said he hadn't heard anyone had died, she explained a man charged by the township with the upkeep of their burial ground had to mow and clear brush now and again. He said he followed her drift and thanked her.

Trudging was getting to be a bother, even around town, as the sun rose higher in an Indian summer sky. So he headed next for the livery.

But as he was crossing the main street he got hailed, and saw it was that bitty little gal who kept the files for old Pete Calhoun. As she fluttered his way like a brown sparrow-bird, waving sheets of yellow foolscap paper, she looked as if she was fixing to flop down in the street and dust-bathe her feathers. She declared she'd been on her way to his hotel after just missing him all the other places he'd been that morning. He believed her. He took the papers from her with a tick of his hat brim, saying, ''There was no need for you to lather yourself like so, ma'am. I take it these are the names and dates I asked your boss for?''

She nodded eagerly and replied, "Everyone who's ever died here in Saddle Rock since it was no more than some tool sheds and telegraph poles surrounded by open range. It wasn't too much bother. As you'll see, we've had less than one death a month since we started keeping records."

Longarm couldn't see reading the lists in the middle of a dusty street, and he owed the hot and flustered little gal for getting all hot and flustered for him. So he nodded at a pink and blue sign up a ways and asked, "Might you care for some ice cream or at least a sip of sarsaparilla with me as I peruse these papers, Miss . . . ?"

She said her friends called her Daisy and she surely would enjoy just a sip of soda before she had to head back to her files. So he offered her an elbow, she took it shyly, and that was where they went.

Nobody laughed as they passed by. Daisy wan't all that ugly, next to some of the nester gals who were in town to shop while their menfolk got drunk, and the henna-rinsed waitress in the corner ice cream parlor kept her thoughts to herself as she sat them in wire chairs at a marble-topped table and served them both the ice cream sodas Longarm suggested as a compromise.

He glanced over the neatly typed lists she'd prepared for him, but it would have been rude to study them right at the table with her. So he didn't, and it only seemed a million years crept by as she gushed on about coming West to seek fame and fortune from some sparrow rookery in Ohio. She seemed to feel typing up mortality lists for the federal authorities was a real adventure. That was what she seemed to think he was, a federal authority. He idly wondered why any gal with so little to offer buttoned her summer-weight bodice so tight. He wondered why a man who wasn't shipwrecked on some lonely island would wonder about a gal who was built like a soft young boy. But he managed to spark back at her just enough to avoid showing how little he enjoyed her tedious company.

113

For he sensed she'd been spurned as tedious by others, male and female, as she'd fluttered through life in a pathetic eagerness to please.

It was starting make him feel awkward by the time she got to all she'd read about him in the *Rocky Mountain News*. So he dropped his eyes to the papers spread beside his soda glass and spotted something it was more modest to talk about.

He said, "I'd heard Slippery Sally O'Shay was dead. But I didn't know she'd died here in Saddle Rock from pneumonia last winter, at least as Dod Kruger saw it."

Daisy sounded a mite catty as she demurred. "There was nothing about anyone called Slippery on any death certificate in our files. Who was this creature and what might she have been to you?"

Longarm smiled soothingly and said, "She wasn't no creature, she was a confidence woman and thief. But she was never federal. I never met up with her, as a sucker or as the arresting officer. I only saw her one time, when Segeant Nolan of the Denver P.D. pointed her out to me in the Union Station and warned me to stick my hand in the same pocket as my wallet and just leave it there in the company of a gal like Slippery Sally O'Shay."

"Was she pretty?" asked the drab little file clerk venomously.

Longarm thought back. "Nice-looking, in an easy-to-forget way. I understand her game was to pick up prosperous strangers as a lonely fellow traveler, and then rob them as they thought they were getting to know her better."

"You mean in the biblical sense," said the little brown file clerk.

It had not been a question. But fair was fair. So Longarm shrugged and replied, "I never asked how far Slippery Sally went with a sucker. I doubt she went further than she needed

114

to. Ladies who prey on foolish men for a living don't seem to admire 'em all that much.''

Daisy seemed to feel he was being too generous.

He told her there was nothing to be gained by speaking ill of the dead, as long as they just stayed dead and didn't traipse all over a small town getting their pictures taken.

He added, ''I see Slippery Sally took sick and died in the very hotel I'm staying at. That's easy to buy, seeing it's the only hotel in town. Deathless Dan Marlow wasn't checked into any proper hotel at the time we sure thought I'd killed him for good. But it might be worth asking the next time I pass through my lobby. Wouldn't it be something if I found a dead man's name on a hotel register?''

She smiled uncertainly and declared she'd never heard of a dead man checking into any hotel.

He said he'd only been funning. Then he fished out his pocket watch and marveled at how late it was getting.

That worked. Daisy said she had to get back to her files too, and slurped the last of her soda through her wheat straw as Longarm let the dregs of his own soda be.

He walked her back to her office, where they shook hands and parted more friendly than Longarm was comfortable with. But what else could a man do when a gal held up her fool wrist to be kissed French-style?

Chapter 12

Longarm rode out of town on a sorrel barb to see how Herb Norman and his hands were coming with that cemetery. The sun was as high as it was going to get this late in the year, but it seemed a tad cooler and far less dusty as they cut across tawny buffalo grass and blue grama just starting to come green at the roots again as the nights got cooler and each day dawned with a tad more dew. Hither and yon he spied some handsome blue-trumpeted hairbell hanging on in the lower draws, as if to remind riders that despite the short-grass prairie all around they were still a good ways up in the sky. To the west, purple peaks of the front range peeked over the horizon as if to confirm what the wildflowers said.

The burial grounds were just outside of town. So that sorrel had only carried Longarm twenty minutes or so before he spied the hedge of box elder sort of marking the boundaries of the cemetery as the white or brownstone markers and handful of mausoleums shimmered in the sun atop the rise beyond.

As he made for the wagon trace that led through the vandalized gate he recalled from before, Longarm spotted another rider to his south, riding the same direction but too far off to be headed for the burial grounds. Longarm reined in and waved a howdy at the distant dot. But nobody waved back. So Longarm said, "Up your own then," and rode on. The other rider might not have spotted him, or might not have been raised to be quite as polite. Some folks thought there was no need to signal peaceable intent to strangers on the range now that the Indians had been run out of these parts. From the way the rude cuss had been riding, he figured to be a cowhand or nester in a hurry. There wasn't any other town to be heading for down that way.

Longarm rode on to the far side of the box elders, and found Herb Norman and two Mexican kids with no trouble. The undertaker was in shirtsleeves but seated on a tombstone, smoking a corncob pipe, as he kept an eye on the two Mexicans. One was whacking at weeds with a grass whip, while the other raked and forked his windrows into a wheelbarrow. Things became clearer as Longarm spotted the weathered wooden stakes lined up where they were clearing. Unlike some bigger towns, Saddle Rock saw no need for a separate potter's field. But that wasn't to say the poor folks buried at public expense got to repose on higher and drier ground amid their social superiors.

Herb Norman told his helpers not to stop as he rose to greet Longarm, asking what had brought him out this way.

Longarm dismounted and tethered the sorrel to a box-elder limb as he replied, "Shaving loose fuzz with Occam's razor. I just got a list from Pete Calhoun's Miss Daisy. It agrees with what you and Doc Kruger say about your healthy climate. But they don't pay me to leave well enough alone."

He got out a cheroot as he nodded at the lonesome wooden stakes and said, "I just now read you'd planted Slippery Sally O'Shay out here somewheres."

Norman took the pipe from his mouth to point at a stake near the uphill edge of that plot, saying, "Yonder. No embalming, but a pine box that'll last as long as all but her bones. What do you expect for fifteen dollars, egg in your beer? How come

117

you called the gal slippery? She just looked dead when we carried her out of that hotel room during a cold snap earlier this year.''

Longarm explained the lady had been a crook with a colorful nickname. Norman shrugged and allowed she might have been prettier when she'd felt better.

Longarm said, ''Doc Kruger signed her over to you as a pneumonia victim, and one or the other of you would have noticed bullet holes or stab wounds. But for the record, are we talking about a nice-looking gal, around thirty-five or so, with a tad of gray in otherwise dark hair?''

Norman thought and decided, ''Her pubic hair was dark brown. That's all you can be sure of with a woman. I just said she might have been a heap prettier if she hadn't coughed herself to death in a feverish bed she'd been puking and pissing in for days before anyone told Doc Kruger she was dying. She didn't have any money in her purse when we got to her. Constable Crabtree figured she'd come up our way to hide out from somebody, ran out of money, and took sick in secret.''

Longarm started to say something dumb, and then he nodded and said, ''Right, Crabtree was killed more recently. So he would have been the one to report what happened to the sheriffs's department in Fort Collins.''

He started to ask something dumb about Crabtree following usual procedure. But then he said, ''If it hadn't been properly reported I'd have never heard about her being dead before I ever got here. So there goes another slice with Occam's razor. Nobody's been taking pictures of the late Slippery Sally anyhow. Let's talk about more important dead folks. Most last wills and testaments include a proviso for a proper funeral, with the expenses to be skimmed off the bulk the estate.''

Herb Norman snorted, ''Tell me something I hadn't heard. I barely do enough business to make ends meet, and I purely never bury anyone who can afford it without asking in advance about who's paying.''

Longarm nodded. ''I admire a man with a good head for figures. How often might you be paid off by an insurance company, or get your money after someone *collects* from such an outfit?''

Norman shook his head. ''Never. I doubt many folks in these parts carry all that much insurance. It costs more than new bobwire or a windmill pump, and folks out this way would rather deal with the here and now whilst the future takes care of its own fool self.''

He glanced at the sun and called out for his Mexican kids to take a work break. As they downed their gear Longarm started to say Kruger had told him much the same. But then one of the kids who were headed to join them shouted, ''*Dios mio, cuidado!*''

So Longarm dropped to the weed stubble, groping for his own gun as another squibbed in the distance and the Mexican who'd been slower to heed his own warning gasped, ''*Ay, mierditas, que pendejada!*'' as he sank to his knees with an expression of numb chagrin and flopped over on on side.

Everyone else had flattened out in the weeds by then, and as Longarm spied gunsmoke against the skyline he yelled, ''Up by Madame Laverne's mausoleum, just like the other night!''

Herb Norman spat out some straw to protest, ''I don't buy that. I can see the bronze door from here and it's shut, damn it!''

Longarm drew a bead and spanged two hundred grains of lead off the bronze just for luck. It sounded something like a big dull Chinese gong talking back to his six-gun.

When nothing else happened Longarm yelled, ''Watch my ass. I want to ask your helper what he saw just now!''

But by the time he'd crawled over to the Mexican, the kid lay dead with a dreamy smile and a mighty bloody shirt. The other Mexican hadn't seen anything before he'd ducked as advised by the dead boy.

Longarm decided, "I might be able to make her up to the crest by working from tombstone to tombstone. I had to cross more open ground than yonder at Shiloh and I still managed."

Herb Norman grimly pointed out how seldom anyone aimed at a particular target all the way across a battlefield. Longarm told him not to be so optimistic. Then he took a deep breath, sprang to his feet, and ran the hundred or so miles uphill to the nearest fair-sized tombstone.

As he flopped in the dry grass behind it Longarm knew the odds weren't likely to improve as he worked closer to the sniper's gun sights. So he emptied his own six-gun at the sky, knowing that one shot wasn't likely to bring any help from the boys back in town.

There came no return fire from the slope above. Longarm still took his time as he reloaded six in the wheel. Then there was nothing he had any good excuse to do but dash on up to a stone angel on a nice square base and make it, again, without drawing fire.

"Cowardly bastard shot and ran!" he muttered aloud, even as he warned himself not to be hasty. He'd seen such confidence take as much as sixty years off a less cautious man's life in his time.

But he drew no fire as he made it to the crest of Signal Rise in a series of ass-puckered dashes. He stood by Madame Laverne's red sandstone mausoleum and waved Herb and the surviving Mexican kid up the slope, yelling, "Fetch that Winchester from my saddle boot, and I'll cover you as you swing wide to scout behind such tombstones as I can't see over from here!"

They did, Herb Norman packing the Winchester at port while his unarmed but thoroughly pissed-off helper moved up at a different angle. When they joined him, Longarm said, "We

120

ought to be having a heap of company directly, unless a lot of jackrabbit hunters fire fusillades in these parts. As long as we're not doing anything up on this slope, what say we have us another look inside this crypt?''

Herb handed Longarm his carbine as he gingerly tried the door latch. He said, ''That killer couldn't have ducked in here. Not without a passkey.''

Longarm handed his revolver to the grim-faced Mexican, levered a round in the chamber of his Winchester, and quietly said, ''Maybe he has one. Let's make sure.''

The undertaker shrugged, got out his key ring, and fitted one key in the lock as he explained, ''These locks come in no more than eight patterns. That's enough to keep the kids out and it saves a heap of fumbling at a bad time for the bereaved.''

Longarm just nodded as the older man cracked the door open and put his back into swinging it wider on its creaky hinges.

The same three coffins had the musty interior to themselves. Herb Norman said, ''Told you nobody was in here.''

Longarm said, ''That ain't entirely true. Let's have us another look in Deathless Dan's coffin.''

Norman blinked and said, ''That's loco, Longarm. We already looked in that box and there was nobody in it, remember?''

Longarm nodded, but insisted, ''That's why I want to look again. It's been my experience that things are often hid the last place anyone would have just cause to look.''

So old Herb put his key ring away and got out his pocket screwdriver as he muttered about suspicious lawmen.

Longarm held out his hand to the Mexican kid for his six-gun as Herb unscrewed the coffin lid. Longarm holstered his gun, but kept the primed Winchester at port while the older man worked.

Then Norman told the Mexican kid to help, and together they lifted the lid off. It was the kid who screamed, dropped his end of the heavy lid, and ran outside as if he'd seen a haunt.

That big gray cat tried to bolt out of Longarm's guts as he saw what had scared the kid like that. Herb just muttered, "Some sneaky son of a bitch had better be able to account for this!"

The object of all the confusion lay grinning up at them from the coffin as if he'd been there all the time. Embalming fluid only did so much for a corpse for so long. So there was little more than dry cracked leather, the color of worn-out boots, holding the skeleton together in its musty ten-dollar suit.

But you could still make out the bushy brows and mummified parrot nose of the sincerely dead Deathless Dan Marlow.

Once help arrived and they got both bodies into town, Doc Kruger said he meant to take his own sweet time before he signed any more death certificates. So Longarm returned the sorrel to the livery, put his saddle gun back in his hotel room, and spent some time at the Western Union before he ambled over to pester Pete Calhoun some more.

Fluttery little Daisy was alone in the office when Longarm got there. She said her boss had left for the day. Longarm wasn't rude enough to observe it was a tad early in the afternoon to start drinking. He told her what he'd come for and asked if she couldn't handle it just as well.

The little brown sparrow fluttered her eyelids up at him and told him, "Good heavens, we've never had a city directory, Custis. Saddle Rock has never been a city."

He said, "I noticed, no offense. Don't you have tax rolls, lists of registered voters, and so forth?"

She shook her head and replied, "Not as complete as all that. The county clerk down to Fort Collins would have all that in his files. I think they send lists of registered voters up this way to our poll watchers come election times. But I don't really know much about voting. Wyoming Territory lets girls vote but

Colorado won't, the mean things."

Longarm started to ask a dumb question. Then he nodded and said, "Right. The county assesses and taxes property. Townships only get township license fees, magistrate's court fines, and so on. You'd only have Saddle Rock society listed as taxpayers or pests."

She said she feared he was right, and asked why he needed the names she just couldn't give him.

He said, "Wanted to see who's living around here, of course. I had 'em show me the hotel records going back a ways. Found the name of a shady lady who died without ever moving on. Found others the room clerk couldn't tell me that much about. Saddle Rock is at the far end of a railroad spur to nowheres else. Folks who stay at the hotel ain't just passing through. They've come up this way on business you'd expect to find some record of, or they've come to stay and were only at that hotel until they got settled in."

He started to reach for a casual smoke, decided he'd better not, and continued. "The room clerk at the hotel has a fair memory, and it ain't as if they've ever been overcrowded since they built the place. So he was able to account for all but handful, including a few with suspicious-sounding names."

She stared up owl-eyed and asked him to repeat some of those suspicious names.

He said, "Smith, Jones, Johnson, and Martin. Most folks don't know what a common name Martin is. But the Martins add up as soon as you consider Martin can be English, Irish, Scotch, French, High or Low Dutch, or even Mex—if you drop the EZ off Martinez. Saint Martin was the popular patron of military men in the old countries.

She said, "I know lots of folks named Smith and such. None of them have ever acted at all suspicious."

He said, "I know. That's doubtless why such common names are so popular with more sinister folks. As that clerk just remarked all too accurately, it's tough to recall whether a strange guest's face went with Smith, Jones, or Johnson. Introduce yourself in a card game as Bob Martin and nobody's likely to be certain who you said you were once the gunsmoke clears.''

She said she only knew one family of Martins in Saddle Rock and that she doubted they shot up card games very often.

He nodded down at her and said that in that case he'd just get on down the road.

But she said, ''I still owe you for that snack this morning. How would you like chicken and dumplings with apple pie for supper?''

He blinked in mingled surprise and dismay as she gushed on about living nearby alone. She'd warned him she'd come West on her own in search of excitement.

He didn't want to hurt such an unexciting little thing. So he got out his notebook to write down her address as he gallantly pointed out that me might not be able to make it that evening. She seemed content with his excuse about coroner's hearings and possible arrests. But of course she wanted to know who he meant to arrest and for what.

Longarm put the notebook away and placed a finger alongside his nose as he winked down and her and soberly declared, ''Wouldn't be fair to accuse anyone right out before I have the evidence for the grand jury, Miss Daisy. But I'm sure I'm getting mighty warm.''

She gasped, ''Ooh, can't you at least tell me what's been going on? I've been listening to the menfolk talk about all this spooky stuff around Saddle Rock and I confess I'm totally at sea!''

He didn't tell her that made two of them. He assured her she'd be told the whole tale in good time, and crawfished out of her little office before she could leap over the desk at him.

He hadn't found out a damned thing he hadn't already known, save that Daisy wanted to cook supper for him as well.

He ambled on up toward Doc Kruger's place, softly singing about the only hymn that he'd ever agreed with all the way. It went:

> Farther along, we'll know more about it,
> Farther along, we'll understand why.
> Cheer up, my brothers, walk in the sunshine,
> We'll understand this, all, by and by.

He surely didn't understand much so far. Every fact he'd been able to gather since he'd left Denver just lay tangled in his brain in a logjam that made no sensible pattern no matter how he wiggled and jiggled certainties and educated guesses around. He told himself to quit guessing and just go with the certain facts he knew. But that was like the fable another pretty Russian lady had told him about the Brotherhood of the Ants. He wondered if old Valya Mirov at the photography place knew that one. She likely did, being Russian herself.

Russian kids were taught they could learn the lingo of the little ants of field and forest and ask them to bring them gold dust, gemstones, and such from under the ground if only they could manage to pass one test. The Brotherhood of the Ants could tell if you cheated. Magic spells were magic. The test called for a boy or girl to go out in the woods and sit on a stump for just one hour without ever, for one full hour, thinking about a big white bear.

That was doubtless why there were so few who'd ever joined that Brotherhood of the Ants. For no matter how he tried to separate wild guesswork from the little he had nailed down, his head was awhirl with fact and fancy that didn't add up worth shit.

He found Herb Norman, Mayor Givens, and Nat Hayward jawing with the deputy coroner on his back porch when he got there. The day was ending warm for Indian summer, and Longarm wasn't anxious to enter the stinky examining room either.

Doc Kruger nodded at Longarm as he joined them and said, "We were just talking about you. Hernando Moreno was killed by a .45-caliber bullet just over the heart. The same as Constable Crabtree."

Longarm shrugged and said, "Same caliber leastways. What about that dried-out cadaver we found in Dan Marlow's coffin?"

Doc Kruger shrugged and replied, "It appears to be Dan Marlow. Same features and gross anatomy. Same suit Herb here put on his embalmed body."

"Slit up the back," the undertaker chimed in. "It's a trade secret. We don't expect 'em to get up and wander about with a bare behind showing. It's a real chore to dress a stiff any other way."

Doc Kruger made a wry face and said, "Makes them easy to undress as well. The Y-shaped incision I made at the time of his first autopsy had gaped open between stitches in places. The only lead we ever found in him was that buckshot you put in him out behind Madame Laverne's, Deputy Long. I found no other wounds, old or fresh, when I examined him again this afternoon."

Longarm dryly remarked, "I never accused a half-mummified corpse of murdering Hernando Moreno or anyone else, Doc."

Kruger said, "In that case I'd better put it down as homicide by a person or persons unknown. Moreno was the only one who saw his killer, for all the good it did him!"

Longarm asked, "What about the other stiff in yonder, Doc?"

Kruger looked bemused. "I suppose he ought to go back where you found him. Madame Laverne paid for his coffin and his crypt and nobody can deny he's dead!"

Longarm demanded, "But where's he *been* all this damned time?"

The deputy coroner smiled wearily and replied, "I can assure you he hasn't been up to any mischief. Any serious attempt to bend one of his limbs would crack it off like a dead tree branch."

Herb Norman swore softly and chimed in with: "*Kids* are the ones who get into mischief this close to Halloween, or hell, most any time you don't watch the little bastards! I'd hate to have this get around, but a year or so ago we caught these schoolkids out at the cemetery after dark, trying to dig up a coffin. They told Constable Crabtree they just wanted to see a skeleton. He told their parents they'd see the interior of that reform school down in Golden if they ever did a thing like that again."

The undertaker spat over the rail and morosely added, "Reckon they were inspired by Crabtree's death to start up again. Wonder what on earth they were doing with that dead outlaw all this time."

Longarm asked for some names to put in his notebook. Mayor Givens demurred. "Those high-spirited boys are all from fine families, Deputy Long."

Longarm said, "John Wesley Hardin's daddy was a minister, Mister Mayor. I don't aim to accuse nobody before I have some evidence to back me up. So I want them names and, oh, yeah, I don't want Deathless Dan put back in his coffin just yet. I want to ask Flash Fleming or Phil Gordon to photograph him some more first."

The three older men exchanged amused glances. The undertaker was the one who said, "You just missed them newspaper boys, old son. They came and went before you got here."

Longarm asked if young Flash had taken any photographs.

Doc Kruger said, "No, they said someone had broken the gadget they use to print photographs with. They have to send back East for some parts. They don't expect to run any photographs in the *Advertiser* this side of Christmas.''

Longarm sighed and said, ''That's another thing Deathless Dan never could have done. I'll ask Phil Gordon. I'll have to pay him, but I'm on an expense account. So what the hell.''

Doc Kruger allowed that the dried-out cadaver would keep well enough in his root cellar for now. Herb Norman had a better idea. It was soon settled he'd fetch his remaining helper and they'd take charge of both dead gents, stale and fresh, as long as they let him embalm and box Moreno before it got messy.

Kruger said he didn't see why Longarm wanted fresh photographs. He pointed out there'd been plenty taken at the time of Marlow's death when he'd looked more natural.

Longarm said, ''I noticed. I know this scientific lady down Denver way who measures dead Indians for the State Historical Society. She can tell you a dead Comanche from a dead Arapaho, albeit she says Arapaho and Cheyenne are too closely related to tell apart by no more than bones.''

The undertaker frowned and said, ''Hold on. Deathless Dan may have been hook-nosed and dark-haired, but he was never any fool Indian!''

Longarm nodded and said, ''I noticed that too. One time this gal who measures bones saved us a whole heap of trouble when she managed to identify some human bones dug up by a dog in a Denver yard as some leftover Arapaho remains from the Shining Times of Mister Lo and his buffalo. I want her to compare close-up photographs of Marlow just after death with fresh ones, shot at the same angle, with his facial bone structure even more pronounced.''

Doc Kruger asked, ''My God, are you suggesting someone has struck us with a mummified ringer that looks like Marlow, was autopsied like Marlow, and has on the same moldy clothing as Marlow?''

Longarm replied simply, "Ain't suggesting nothing. I want to *know*. The only thing certain about this confusion is that the gent we brought in off Signal Rise this afternoon can't be the one who shot Constable Crabtree a few short days ago, or Hernando Moreno this very afternoon."

Chapter 13

Phil Gordon wasn't at his gallery. Valya Mirov said he'd gone to a wedding over in Buckeye with his best box camera. She didn't know when he'd be back. Buckeye was about a two-hour drive each way, and you never knew about wedding receptions.

When Longarm told her what he wanted, she said she'd be proud to help out. She hung a sign in the door glass explaining they were closed, and fetched another camera, a tripod, and such. Longarm said he'd carry, and she never argued. The damned gear was more awkward than heavy. By the time they got over to Herb Norman's he was sorry he'd been too lazy to hire a buckboard.

Old Herb was working on the dead Mexican inside. But he came out to show them where he and his other helper had stored Deathless Dan in a shed, standing up in a corner amid bales of bobwire and fence posts.

As Valya set up her tripod in the sunny yard, Longarm and Norman hung Deathless Dan on a nail in the shed door by the collar of his shabby suit. It was easy. Like most folks, the outlaw had been seventy-percent water when he'd died. So now his dried skin and bones weighed less than a hundred pounds.

Valya captured his grim new image in glass as Longarm swung the shed door between shots to get him at more than one angle. Then Longarm had an even grander notion, and got the immigrant gal to take Dan's picture, then move her tripod just a yard to the right and take the same picture, almost. She understood better than the undertaker when Longarm explained, "Might be able to fashion one of them stereoscope cards that makes things look more real."

Herb Norman smiled and asked, "Is that how they make them magic views that look as if you could reach out and touch things in the photographs you know full well to be flat? Well, I never, and I sure admire modern science. You figure that scientific gal in Denver may be able to judge things better viewed in depth, right?"

Longarm said that was about the size of it. Valya slid the negative case out and dropped it into its wooden holding case as she asked what Longarm wanted her to try next.

He said, "May as well hang him back in the cool shade and develop what we have, Miss Valya. We've all we need if someone better at the science than us is really that much better. If it ain't possible to prove my point scientifically, a dozen more pictures ain't likely to help."

He helped old Herb put the body away again for now. Herb asked when he could stick Deathless Dan back in his permanent address up on Signal Rise. Longarm started to object, then shrugged and said the body seemed safer behind a bronze door in a stone mausoleum than just hanging around.

Heading back out front, Herb asked who Longarm figured might take Deathless Dan for another walk.

Longarm grimaced and said, "Same ones who did it the last time. Do you see dead folks walking about on their *own* all that often?"

"Wouldn't make much sense," Norman said. "That body inside was gutted like a chicken, and such brawn as Deathless

131

Dan ever had has been dried to strings of jerky. So how could the ugly cuss wander all over town like a live human, having his fool picture took?''

Longarm said they were still working on that. Then he gathered up Valya and her gear and trudged them back to her photography gallery as the shadows commenced to lengthen in the golden sunlight.

It was just far enough for Longarm to casually bring up the subject of Valya's boss, Phil Gordon. He said he didn't want her to get in any trouble acting on her own like this again.

She didn't seem to know what he was talking about. He chose his words, but managed to repeat some of the dumb conversation about her that he'd had with her boss.

Valya chuckled fondly and said, ''Poor he. I think he really wants to marry me. The first time he proposed and I said *nyet* I thought I was going to be looking for other job. But Phil never says anything cross to me. Sometimes I think he would pay me if I did nothing but stand out front of door and smile, *nyet*?''

Longarm smiled thinly and said, ''Some gents are like that when they're really fond of a gal. He seems a good old boy, and his intentions toward yourself seem honorable to the point of pathetic, no offense. I don't reckon you'd care to tell me why he seems to making such poor progress, ma'am?''

Valya shrugged her small shoulders as she took two steps to his one and explained, ''Ask me why I don't fall in love with faithful dog or friendly cat. I *like* Phil. He had been most kind to me since I came to him for job I badly needed. He has been, how you say, good sport about my refusal to marry him, or even let him kiss me at door when he is walking me home after dark. I told him would not be fair to either of us. He said he does not understand. Maybe that is why would not be fair to either of us, *da*?''

Longarm allowed he followed her drift. He didn't ask her

132

who she'd left, or lost, in her old country. Some kindly old philosopher had once observed, doubtless in French, that a man was a fool to chase after gals who'd given their hearts to others in a world where most gals wore their hearts on their sleeves. He knew Phil Gordon would be likely to take a swing at him if he ever suggested as much. So he wasn't fixing to, and wasn't life a bother, until you considered the alternatives.

Back at the studio, Valya left the sign on the door so nobody'd disturb them, they hoped, while she developed and printed the plates she'd just taken.

He had a safer suggestion. He said, "I'd best stay out on the walk whilst you work alone in your darkroom, Miss Valya. Like you said, Buckeye is only a two-hour drive, and they usually serve strong drink at big weddings."

She was smart as she looked. So she nodded gravely and told him, "I will take hour or more, and Phil is still going to say silly things if he thinks you wait for me out front to take for buggy ride. So why you not go for supper and come back around sundown, *nyet*?"

That sounded mighty sensible. He agreed, and she let him out before she locked the door after him. He checked the time, and strode along the walk to that beanery near his hotel.

Keeping an eye on the time, he ordered and enjoyed a lollygagging supper from onion soup to their special of roast beef, string beans, and a mashed potato volcano spewing buttered gravy lava from its artistic crater. When he told the ash-blond waitress how much he admired their cook's imagination, she said she'd done that with the spuds and that she got off at nine.

Saddle Rock was surely blessed with young gals who'd come West for some excitement. It was sort of sad to see them stuck in a town that was getting to be so slow, save for dead folks who seemed to be looking for action.

As he ate his mince pie he told himself not to think about dead folks pestering the living. Such goings-on made no sense

133

in a rational set of plans by a sane creator. He remembered reading about those Salem witch trials that had gotten all out of hand before one old Puritan judge had just shaken his head and declared he'd heard just about enough of that shit about curses and devils and little screaming children pointing at things nobody else could see. Salem was the one time and place in history where the deluded but well-meaning witch hunters themselves had finally said, "Aw, shit, I just don't buy any more of this!"

He washed down the overly rich pie with black coffee, paid off the artistic waitress, and left her a dime tip to show he hadn't been disgusted by her offer.

Another kindly philosopher had warned him there'd be nights like this. Women sensed when a man had other plans just as keenly as a shark sensed blood in seawater, and it seemed to have the same effect on both man-hunting critters.

It was closer to sundown now, and the light was getting tricky as he drifted slowly back towards Gordon's Gallery lest Valya, or worse yet her boss, suspect him of being eager.

He reached for a cheroot as he cheerfully considered how tough it could be to get laid in a town this dinky when a man had nothing else on his mind. He'd had no idea he'd run into Edwina Chaffee and her outfit up this way. That other time he'd ridden with her he'd gotten nowhere at all. That was likely the reason she'd almost raped him the other night.

He'd have surely just made Iris Jane from the schoolhouse cry if he'd had slap and tickle in mind from the beginning. Women sure had instincts, and just acting like you didn't care didn't fool them either. He remembered that time he'd met the lovely Ellen Terry during her acting company's Western tour, and how he'd managed not to jerk off or even drool as they were introduced at that party after the show. He was certain he'd kept a poker face as Reporter Crawford of the *Denver Post* introduced them. But Miss Terry had still smiled graciously and stared right through him as if he'd been a dumb schoolboy instead of a grown man shaking hands with one of the few gals on earth he'd be willing to marry up with and cherish forever.

"Asshole," he called himself as he paused in front of a closed shop to light his cheroot. For he knew Ellen Terry was over thirty, and a foreigner besides. Sure, she was beautiful, gracious, and charming. But so were a lot of gals. So he decided it was the intelligent look in her steady eyes. He suspected a gal that wise and worldly would be swell to talk to in bed, and capable of coming up with some original positions as well. But she was doubtless in love with some lime-juicing earl who liked to use and abuse her, so what the hell.

He almost bumped into an old lady on the walk, and excused himself with a sincere sweep of his Stetson, saying, "I didn't see you, ma'am. This orange and purple time of the day plays trick on our eyes. Or on my eyes leastways."

The old lady just sniffed and brushed on past, as if she'd thought he was trying to be forward, for God's sake.

He chuckled and moved on, having trouble with his cheroot in the evening breezes. Sometimes they just rolled a blamed smoke wrong on you, and there were times a man could waste more money on waterproof matches from Old Mexico than a blamed three-for-a-nickel mistake was worth.

He paused under an awning, out of the breeze, to get rid of the one and light another. As he did so he heard two gunshots from down the way he was headed. He frowned thoughtfully, got rid of the match, and strode on. He saw another gent, dressed more cow, headed his way but walking in the dust of the street in such gloaming light as there was. So Longarm stepped out into the same light, lest he surprise a stranger packing his own six-gun low, and cheerfully said, "Howdy! Was that gunplay I heard just now?"

The other man, his own features shaded by his wider hat

brim, dropped into a gunfighting crouch and went for his gun!

Longarm beat him to the draw. It wasn't easy. As Longarm blew the wild cuss off his feet and then shot the .45 he'd dropped halfway across the street with a more carefully aimed round, he threw down on the writhing wretch at his feet and snorted, "You're supposed to draw and *then* bend your knees like so, old son. Where'd I nail you?"

The rider on the ground groaned, "I'm shot in the guts and I'll never forgive either one of us! They told me you were good, but Jesus H. Christ, that was pure impossible!"

Others were cautiously edging closer as Longarm fumbled out his badge and pinned it to a lapel, declaring he was the law and wanted a doctor *poco tiempo*

Then he eased over to hunker by the stranger he'd shot, casually asking, "To what might I owe this honor, old son? Your face is familiar, but I don't recall us being at feud."

The man he'd gutshot groaned, "Well, we are, you fancy Romeo from the big city. I told Miss Edwina you was only trifling with her and she up and fired me! What do you *do* to them, lick pussy, you good-for-nothing pimp?"

Longarm had no call to pistol-whip a dying man. So he didn't, but it wasn't easy as the cuss he now recalled from Edwina Chaffee's cow camp pissed and moaned a tale of unrequited lust. Doc Kruger joined them, followed shortly by Sid Marner, who helped a heap by yelling for everyone else to stay back as the country doctor cum deputy coroner hunkered down with them. Nat Hayward came across the street at an angle, asking what was up.

Longarm said, "I just put this lovelorn fool down. What was he shooting at down the street, before I asked him and came close to getting my face blown away?"

The young constable said, "I don't know. I was headed that way when I heard you shooting up this way. You say you know him, Longarm?"

The lawman who'd almost paid with his life for knowing the idiot's boss lady better nodded gravely and said, "He just blamed me for his getting fired."

Then he turned to Kruger to ask, "What are his chances, Doc?"

Before Kruger could answer there came an anguished womanly wail from way down the street. So Longarm was up and running, with the two local lawmen right behind him.

As they approached Phil Gordon's Gallery, they saw an even bigger crowd gathered around the entrance. As Longarm bulled through he saw that the wails, in Russian, were coming from Valya Mirov.

She had Phil Gordon's head cradled in her lap in the tricky light.

Longarm dropped to one knee beside her and felt for a pulse as he quietly asked her what had happened.

She sobbed, "I am not knowing! I was in darkroom, developing prints, when I hear shot like last night! I keep door locked until I hear all others yelling out here. Then I know is safe to come out. So I come out and Phil is lying in doorway, shot in back. I ask him what happen and he is saying he loves me. That is all I am knowing!"

Longarm gently told her, "You know he's got to say what he had in mind at the end, Miss Valya. For I fear he's never going to say another word. I wish there was a nicer way to put it, but there ain't. He's dead."

Chapter 14

This time the coroner's hearing was a real gully-washer, with the county sending people up from Fort Collins to back Doc Kruger's play, a brace of experienced investigators from the sheriff's department, and an observer from the state police. Billy Vail wired permission for Longarm to lay over longer, seeing he was a material witness as well as the only federal law in these parts.

That circuit judge who'd been holding court over in Buckeye wired Doc Kruger to hold off until he could swing over Saddle Rock way, but everyone else agreed they might as well get cracking, and Doc Kruger called the meeting to order the next day in the school auditorium. For three killings in the same damned day had talking about the weather beat all to hell, and the one hotel had never done so much business since they'd built her with an optimistic number of rooms for a town that size.

But once Doc Kruger had pounded some order in the crowded barnlike chamber, with Doc and the other panelists seated up on stage behind a trestle table like they were posing for the Last Supper, things went a tad swifter than some present

138

might have expected when they'd hitched up for the drive into town.

For such eyewitness testimony as they had on tap was terse and undisputed. Longarm, Herb Norman, and the surviving Mexican kid, Verdugo, told the same simple story about the shooting of Hernando Moreno. It seemed clear the dead boy had spotted the shootist throwing down on them from up around the Laverne mausoleum and shouted that warning just as he himself was getting shot. Nobody else had had seen anything up yonder but some drifting smoke. When Longarm tried to interest them in the late Deathless Dan, there came a wave of nervous laughter, and Doc Kruger rapped for order and declared, "Let's not get sidetracked with graveyard humor. I examined that dead outlaw nigh three years ago, and then again just yesterday. On both occasions he was dead, and this hearing was called to determine the cause of more recent deaths."

Longarm said, "I know. I cheerfully confess to killing Poker Zeke Warner out of Texas by way of the Chaffee spread down Leadville way. But Hernando was gunned within sight of Deathless Dan's tomb, and Phil Gordon had more than one photograph of Deathless Dan taken recently. Don't that add up to *something,* Doc?"

Kruger smiled uncertainly and demanded, "If so, what? A badly preserved drawn and drained cadaver busting out of its coffin to shoot three men, counting Constable Crabtree a spell back, with the same .45 army short slugs?"

Longarm grimaced and said, "We didn't find a .45 Schofield or any other weapon in Marlow's coffin with his corpse. But it's a common sort of weapon, and there's no proof Poker Zeke used his own Schofield on anyone else before he came at me with it last night."

One of the riders for the sheriff's department frowned down at Longarm and said, "Let's talk about that shootout we have a few more solid facts about, Deputy Long. We've gotten a reply to our own wire from that cadaver's former boss, Miss Edwina Chaffee, over in Masonville where she has her outfit at the moment. She tells us she did fire Zeke Warner for impertinence, which I gather means an unwelcome advance, right here in Saddle Rock as she and her other riders were pulling out. Do you have anything additional you'd care to say about that, seeing you met Zeke Warner earlier out behind your hotel in the Chaffee camp?''

Longarm shook his head and allowed he had nothing he cared to say about Edwina Chaffee, save that she was a good old gal who'd never gun anyone without just cause, and certainly wouldn't fire a man she'd hired to gun somebody for her.

He continued. ''I've chawed and spit that notion out. I can't see as pure hard feelings betwixt Poker Zeke and myself could have inspired him to murder Phil Gordon. I didn't know they *knew* one another. Miss Valya Mirov, who worked for Gordon, told me last night, after we had her calmer, she'd never seen Poker Zeke's dead face before, alive or on photographic paper.''

The white-haired old-timer from the state police took the pipe out of his mouth to pontificate, ''Keeping an open mind on that earlier gunplay that cost Constable Crabtree's life, I see the rapid-fire events of yesterday as simple. We've established the late Poker Zeke Warner was a hot-tempered Texican with a personal grudge. For sensible or less than sensible causes he blamed Deputy Long there for costing him his job and the admiration of a boss lady he had a hankering for. He was almost surely the wicked rascal who throwed a fire-bomb through Long's very window the night he got fired. When that didn't kill anybody, he commenced to stalk his intended victim, working himself up to less cowardly methods.''

Longarm started to object. But the old coot's reconstruction seemed sort of plausible so far.

The older lawman smugly continued. "Deputy Long allows he spied a distant rider who might have been out to head him off at that graveyard. As I reconstruct the shooting out yonder from our diagrams, I make it a barely possible pistol shot from the crest of Signal Rise to where the intended victim was jawing with Herb Norman and his hired help. A .45 revolver in good condition will carry up to four hundred yards, but not with a lick of accuracy past fifty, so—"

"Beg pardon," Longarm said. "A solid-frame Colt .45 will throw a round four hundred yards. But you'd be lucky to lob a lead a hundred with a Schofield loaded with a .45-28 army shorts."

His elder sniffed and said, "Whatever. You couldn't get this child to pack a loose-jointed Schofield to a tea party. But it's a given that the late Poker Zeke was stupid, and that round Hernando Moreno stopped with his chest was fired downhill, from no more than a hundred yards. My point about accuracy was that the killer had no way of making certain who he'd *hit* at that range. So let's agree it was just as likely yourself he was aiming at and get on to the tricky light of gloaming."

Longarm had no call to answer as he pictured Poker Zeke coming at him in the gathering dusk.

The older lawman went on. "He missed you out at the grave-yard and lit out like the coward he was born. Later that same evening—we know from the boys at the saloon how he'd spent the afternoon—he screwed up his nerve to come after you again. Someone must have told him you spent time at the photographer's, and he was likely drunk enough to mistake the tall but harmless Phil Gordon for you in the doorway of his shop. You were both wearing suits and broad-brimmed hats, and we are not accusing a college professor of stalking either of you. He shot Phil Gordon in the back, thinking it was you, and then he ran smack into you again, he thought, as he was fleeing the scene of his crime. You testify yourself he let out a startled gasp and slapped leather the moment he saw you there, just up the way from where he'd killed you, he thought.''

More than one in the crowd chuckled as they pictured how chagrined the backshooting bastard must have felt just before he'd died, trying to do it all over again from scratch.

Doc Kruger rapped for order and told Longarm, ''You'd best stand aside and let us tidy up any details the others on our list may have to offer.''

Longarm protested he wasn't sure things had been that simple. But he was overruled, and they called Sid Marner forward to sit down and tell about his hearing gunplay in the gloaming and running down the street to find Longarm alive and Poker Zeke dying.

Longarm moved over to the open doorway to light a cheroot as he leaned against the jamb. Valya Mirov joined him there, her sloe eyes worried as she timidly asked, ''Is over for me? I felt so awkward as they asked me personal questions about poor Phil and me.''

He took the cheroot from his teeth and assured her, ''Nobody thinks what you're afraid they might be thinking, Miss Valya. I put it down in the report they'd have read before they called you that you were staying at that boardinghouse while your bachelor boss dwelt blocks away, in a town too small for much late-night scampering.''

She smiled like Miss Mona Lisa and murmured, ''I know. Iris Jane thought nobody noticed when she came in just before dawn the other morning. I wonder who she spent most of night with. Don't you?''

Longarm took a drag on his cheroot and blew it out his nostrils to get his voice steadier before he replied, ''I've never been one for such gossip. Let's talk about your own reputation some more. I had no call to record all them mushy things old Phil said about you. Albeit he'd told me himself he was serious. So I don't find it all that surprising he left you his business and cottage up the slope. But I understand he had a life-insurance policy naming you as the sole beneficiary?"

She nodded wistfully and replied, "Poor he. I knew he liked me. I never knew he liked me so much. He never told me about insurance. I only heard last night, when Pete Calhoun came to tell me about last will and testament filed with township. Do I have to go to this Omaha to ask for insurance money? They say Phil had mortgage loan on business and I have no money to pay at beginning of month!"

Longarm explained how they'd likely send her Phil's insurance payoff, after some paperwork. He said, "They'd rather have the interest on the money in their bank account than your own. But they'll have to pay off sooner or later, unless they can prove Phil killed himself, or you did."

She gasped. "How can you say that? Was inside, locked in darkroom with work I was doing for *you,* when somebody shot Phil out on street!"

He said soothingly, "Simmer down. They're about to find Phil was shot in the back by the late Poker Zeke, and you'll have that down on paper if the insurance dicks try to chisel you. I'll point that out when I see if I can wrangle you an extension on your mortgage. Who'd Phil borrow from, Mayor Givens' bank?"

She said, "*Da,* is only bank in town, *nyet*?"

He patted her shoulder and said, "I'm sure he'll be a sport, Miss Valya. I'll tell him you're good for the money as soon as they pay off in Omaha, and meanwhile, what would he want with an empty Gordon's Gallery, even if he has a lien on all your equipment? It ain't as if they'd find a ready market for any shut-down business in a town this slow, you know."

She sighed and said she knew that full well from keeping the books for her dead boss. She allowed they'd barely been making ends meet, and he agreed it would make as much sense for her to sell out and go somewhere folks had more to spend

143

on their portraits. When he saw the thought had just struck her, he said, "Don't sign nothing before I scout the shark-infested waters for you, Miss Valya. It's entirely possible you'd come out ahead if you let them foreclose on a mortgage you never signed and just headed for greener pastures with that insurance nest egg!"

She dimpled up at him and called him a *volkhv,* and added that the Czar was lucky nobody that sneaky was plotting against *him.* He got her to explain a *volkhv* was something like a wizard or warlock, and they agreed to get together later at the photograph studio.

She'd no sooner left him alone in the doorway than Iris Jane came over to pout that she was feeling neglected and couldn't see what he saw in that fat immigrant gal.

Longarm told her soothingly, "We were talking about her testimony at this hearing, honey. I asked them earlier if they wanted you to take the witness chair about that picture you took out front of the schoolhouse. But they said not to be silly. If you were listening just now, you head me try to bring up that restless outlaw Deathless Dan."

She said, "I'll bet her old gash is loose and stinky. I don't want to talk about dead outlaws or their damned doubles. I want you to tell me why you haven't come sparking since I gave you my all and you said I was the best lay in town!"

He softly assured her, "You *are* the best lay in town, as far as I am in any position to declare, and keep your sweet voice down lest a heap of others make the same observation. I never came by last night because I was trying to protect your rep, honey. How would it look if a man just gunned another down on the streets of town and then took a schoolmarm out promenading along those same streets?"

She looked mollified, and declared that in that case he was forgiven and when might she expect some of that grand loving again.

He tried to look sincere as he told her he wasn't sure, explaining he'd already picked up some gossip about her late hours, and pointing out that everyone in town seemed to have their eyes on him.

She laughed, said they'd be shocked if they ever saw him with his pants down, and agreed to let him decide when it would be prudent to get perverse with her some more.

As others commenced to to drift by, he saw the meeting was busting up, and went back to the stage to make sure he had the panel's findings straight.

He didn't. When Doc Kruger told him they'd wrapped up the deaths of all concerned in one neat package called Poker Zeke Warner, Longarm protested. "Hold on! Constable Crabtree was killed way before the firing of a forward cowboy the other night!"

A sheriff's deputy from Fort Collins chimed in to say, "We thought about that, Longarm. No offense, but you might not have been the sole object of a deranged killer's affections. The Chaffee outfit was in these parts when Crabtree was killed and—"

"Rein in and back up," Longarm said, "I got it from Edwina Chaffee in the flesh they'd only been here in Larimer County this fall, buying a cow here and another yonder. Hadn't we better check with her on the whereabouts of her crew at the time everyone says Crabtree was shot on a Saturday night by someone who looked like someone else?"

The county lawman shook his head and said, "There's always a few loose ends. Nobody could say King Henry cut off his wives' heads if they went to talking about what time of the day the headsman put his blade to the grindstone."

Doc Kruger pointed out, "You were the one who noticed how tough it was to get an exact description of Crabtree's killer."

The sheriff's man said, "There you go. A thirsty rider could

145

make it to town from most anywhere in the county in a hard day's ride. If he told his boss lady he'd been out hunting strays instead of getting laid, she'd hardly recall it exactly now. Say he came in to visit that infamous whorehouse of Madame Laverne, found she and her girls had been run out of town, and went after the town law he held responsible for his unsatisfied hard-on.''

Longarm started to object, but had to allow to himself that a man who'd go after one lawman to avenge a frustrated pecker might do almost any fool thing that fit the overall picture.

Kruger said, ''There's nobody else to hang all this wild stuff on. Up until recently, this whole neck of the woods has been pinching its own ass to stay awake. We just don't have any other suspects with a crazy-mean streak and a Schofield .45. Thanks to you and your .44-40, the whole distressing mess seems to be over!''

Longarm quietly asked, ''What if it ain't? What somebody else stops an army short, or even spies that infernal Deathless Dan around town some more?''

The county lawman said, ''We'll posse up and try to cut sign, of course. What the deputy coroner here keeps trying to pound into your head is that everyone else is satisfied for now. The killings have all been accounted for. Haunting ain't usually the concern of any sober soul who packs a badge. If you don't want to send for them Fox sisters back East, your best bet would be to write them odd photographs off as odd photographs. Some jasper who looks something like that dead outlaw was just passing through town.''

Longarm frowned and demanded, ''Then how come I can't find anyone who can tell me who he might be, and what he's been up to in this tiny trail town? Sorry, Doc, but facts are facts, and it ain't as if this was that square in London Town where everyone in the world is sure to pass by if you'd like to wait a spell. I've asked high and I've asked low, at the one

146

hotel, the handful of saloons, and the railroad stop. I showed folks his pictures, dead and alive, and nobody owns up to having seen him in either condition since he lay on that cellar door a good three winters back. Yet there he was at that hotel fire just the other night. So where's he at right now? I'm mighty dubious about that being the same cuss hanging in Herb Norman's tool shed at the moment.''

Doc Kruger nodded soberly and said, "I'd stake everything I ever learned in medical school on *that*! I agree with my fellow county man here, it's simply a chance resemblance.''

Before Longarm could reply, the county law pointed out, "Being a lone wolf nobody knows ain't no crime until you do something, alone or in company, that constitutes a felony. Say that for some reason of his own this mysterious jasper goes out of his way to avoid making friends. Say he drinks standing up in a saloon, watches kids having class pictures taken, or goes to fires without asking our permission. What's he *done* that would justify an arrest?''

Longarm said, "You've both skimmed over that earlier shootout in the cemetery the other night. Your new Constable Hayward got off luckier than Constable Crabtree. But if Nat ain't interested in why he got shot by someone lurking in Dan Marlow's tomb, *I* surely am! I aim to find that double, twin, or whatever and have a serious talk with him about .45 slugs, empty coffins, and such.''

Doc Kruger smiled wryly and said, "Bring him by when you catch up with him and I'll examine him for buckshot free. Herb Norman says he's had trouble with cemetery pranksters before. I'd believe some kids at some time or other stole a mummified corpse, to keep in some cave as a mascot, and then smuggled it back when they heard we were looking for it, before I'll believe the dead rascal climbed out of his box to wound young Nat and chase after fire bells!''

The county law nodded in agreement and asked, "Say you

do catch up with this spooky lookalike and he just tells you to go to Hell? He'd have every right to, you know. Nobody saw him climb out of any damn coffin to do toad squat. If looking spooky was a local, state, or federal offense, I'd have arrested a bunch of my in-laws a long time ago. Let it go, old son. Whoever the cuss was, he ain't around town this afternoon and there's not a bit of solid evidence connecting him to any crime or, hell, misdemeanor!''

So Longarm left the schoolhouse. But he wasn't ready to let it go. Hence he was leg-sore and half convinced by the time he joined a worried Valya Mirov in that darkroom. For he'd been all over town and jawed with all sorts of folks without a lick of luck. It was as if that mysterious stranger had never existed, save for his fool face turning up in photographs taken all over Saddle Rock.

The nine-by-twelve print Valya had developed from the pieced-together newpaper photograph was a pisser, with the spitting image of Deathless Dan Marlow clear as anything, thanks to Valya having done something tricky with the exposure. By overdeveloping the flash photograph shot at night to where Longarm, the fire chief, and Mayor Givens looked a tad washed out, she'd captured an almost portrait-quality image of the rascal standing in the crowd behind them. She said she could touch up the picture to get rid of the cracks. He shook his head and told her it would do fine the way it was.

He explained, "No cracks run across anyone's face, and I only want to show this one ugly mutt to possible witnesses."

She brightened and suggested it might be better if she was to "crop" and enlarge the one important face in the picture. He started to say that would be needless bother. Then he decided showing just a face at such a time had explaining all those others in the print beat.

So she got right to it as he watched, admiring her skilled little hands as she proceeded to turn a cracked-up group picture into just the one ugly face in an almost life-sized enlargement. It was ever so much of an improvement that he asked if she could do the same with other glass negatives on file, cropping out everything but the head and shoulders of everything they had of the rascal.

She said she'd be proud to, and as she worked he told her all he'd found out about her own likely future.

He said, "Mayor Givens was a big help this afternoon. We were right about his bank holding the mortgage on this business, and he sold Phil that insurance too, operating as an agent for the big Omaha outfit that underwrote it."

Longarm got out his notebook and squinted in the ruby light to be sure of his figures as he continued. "Phil took out the mortgage before he ever hired you. He had to. He didn't have that much when the Demille sisters put the place on the market. They're alive and well down Pueblo way, in case you were worried about the original owners. You told me yourself why most would want to set up shop in a bigger town. But Phil must have figured Saddle Rock was riding the wave of the future. So he borrowed the purchase price and some seed money, and they let him use this going business as security."

He thumbed through the dim notes, decided it was a lost cause, and said, "I told you Mayor Givens would be a sport about extending you more credit in your hour of need. Seeing he knows for a fact you'll be coming into ten thousand dollars from that insurance company."

"That much?" she said, thunderstruck. "How could poor he have afforded such insurance?"

Longarm explained. "It was just a simple policy, with double payment for accidental or violent death. That's about as good a deal as anyone can get on life insurance, albeit not for his ownself exactly. Had he poisoned himself from those fumes from that stinky old sink, you'd have only collected five thousand, which wouldn't have been so bad considering your monthly mortgage payments."

She said he could switch on the overhead bulb and open the door to air the place out now. So he did as she hung the enlargements up to dry.

He moved over to admire her work. The enlarged prints were spooky as all get-out. He said, "Look at that wisp of gray in the sideburn of this dead cuss on the cellar door three winters ago. Now tell me I don't see that very same thing in this newspaper picture shot just the other night! And look at those nose hairs sticking out of that same parrot nose. That has to be the very same face, dead or alive!"

Valya made the sign of the cross backwards Russian-style, and almost sobbed, "*Nyet,* is not possible! Peasants tell of such things in *byliny* tales of olden times when *chernobogi* roamed the night on demon horses with eight legs!"

She looked so scared and such a long way from home, he felt it only right to take her in his arms and kiss her.

She kissed back, warm and tender enough to make him feel mighty sorry for poor Phil Gordon. Then he reflected on how honorable his own intentions could afford to be toward any defenseless gal, and let go stiffly, saying, "Don't let nobody do that till you know what you aim to do with the rest of your life, Miss Valya."

She leaned in closer to stare up adoringly with her big slanted eyes and assure him she felt a lot warmer toward him than her late boss, poor he.

Longarm sighed and said, "Phil could have given you a heap more, as slow as business has been. All I have to offer anyone is an occasional night of slap and tickle, a heap more nights of lonesome worry, and mayhaps a modest widow's pension earlier than planned. I've been to too many departmental funerals to saddle a decent gal with my uncertain future, Miss Valya. I've had this wistful sort of conversation before, and I reckon

150

I *may* settle down some day, when I won't have to send word I won't be home for supper because they want me to posse up. But I reckon me and these photographs of a haunt had best be on our way.''

She asked if that meant he was leaving town. To which he could only reply, ''I got to. This spook I'm after ain't here, and they keep ordering me back to Denver. But I sure thank you for asking, ma'am.''

Chapter 15

The train ride back to Fort Collins seemed to take forever, and Longarm's pocket watch warned he was going to miss his transfer to the main line if they didn't get a move on. But when he bitched to the conductor, he was told he was lucky he didn't have to walk.

The conductor added, "The line's been losing money on this spur. They built it with a view to more trade than Saddle Rock ever had. Nesters crowd the country up, and that results in more goods and services. But as you can see out the window, this rolling range hasn't tempted many homesteaders. Cow folk are more spread out and inclined to order way less from the mail-order houses back East."

Longarm allowed he'd noticed things seemed quiet up at the end of the line, save for recent gunplay and haunts. Then he read his magazine over again until at last, by slow huffs and puffs, their antiquated Baldwin General got him and his baggage into Fort Collins a good six minutes after his Denver-bound Burlington had left.

After he'd finished cussing and started another cheroot, he went to the stationmaster's office to make sure. They told him that was indeed the last train for Denver that evening. So he left his saddle and possibles with the baggage clerk and went to supper as he pondered the possible ways to kill a whole night in Fort Collins.

Like Fort Wayne, Fort Worth, and other old forts, Fort Collins had grown to a fair-sized town after the army had decided it didn't need the land anymore. But while Fort Collins was the county seat and far bigger than Saddle Rock, there'd be a lot less going on after dark than at, say, Seventeenth and Larimer in Denver.

Fortified by pumpkin pie and extra black coffee, Longarm wired his reasons for not getting back as quickly as directly ordered, and got out his notebook to see if he could combine some duty with a lot less to do in these parts.

He sent some wires he'd been meaning to send from Denver after talking over the past few days with Billy Vail. Then he left that Western Union to prowl the county seat.

Rank had its privileges, and he wasn't surprised to find their county clerk had already gone home to supper. But he got a musty old file clerk who smoked cheroots to stay open just late enough to let a lawman jot down a few names and dates.

They didn't disagree all that much with what Pete Calhoun and his fluttery sparrow-bird had let him look at up Saddle Rock way. Few folks had been dying and damned little property had been changing hands for a community in the grip of master criminals.

As he left the hall of records perplexed, he recalled what that cowhand had recalled about haunted candy stores. Most of the shops here in Fort Collins stayed open as late as sundown. But he struck out at the first four places he tried.

He figured he was going to again when the older gal behind the fifth candy counter stared blankly at the photograph prints he showed her and declared that while she doubted she could ever forget such an ugly face, she'd never served anyone who'd looked at all like that.

Longarm sighed and said, "I was hoping I'd struck paydirt when I saw you sold violet preserves, ma'am."

He was fixing to walk on out when she smugly replied, "We're the only shop in town that does. They come all the way from Paris, France, and they say the Divine Sarah Bernhardt won't eat anything else."

Longarm smiled thinly and managed not to brag about knowing for a fact that the lady in question cooked and ate her own onion soup. He said, "No offense, but what you just said leaves me confounded, ma'am. I was told by this nice young cowboy that he'd been standing in line for some violet preserves while he watched the spooky-looking cuss in these photographs pestering you about some Chinese lady."

The shopkeeper blinked and demanded, "Is this some sort of cowboy humor? I doubt we've sold candy to a full dozen Chinese *men,* and I've never *seen* the female of that species."

Longarm insisted, "Nobody said you had. The mysterious stranger was the one hunting Chinese in Fort Collins, ma'am. But as you just now suggested, such a conversation as well as such a face ought to lodge in one's memory. So I'll take your word you never met up with the cuss. Save for that one cowboy, he's been mighty elusive no matter who I ask."

He thanked her as he put the pictures away. Then, as he was turning to leave, another notion struck him. It would have been rude to say the gal behind the counter seemed a mite old to be called a *gal* by a cowhand young enough to be her son. So he simply asked if she was the only lady who'd ever sold violet preserves there.

The nice old woman shook her gray head and replied, "I should have thought of Miss Simmons myself, for heaven's sake. She's a neighborhood dressmaker who fills in for me from noon to one while I go home for dinner. She says it's a welcome break in her own day as well. Is it possible *she* was behind this counter when your informant saw this suspicious character in here?''

Longarm said there was only one way to find out. So the shopkeeper gave him a business card, explaining how Miss Martha Simmons drummed up a little business of her own while waiting on female customers in the candy store.

Longarm figured out the address, up a side street but not too far, and got there just as someone was lighting a lamp behind the lace curtains of a bay window.

He mounted the wooden steps to the front door and twisted the door-chime knob. The thirty-year-old gal who came to the door had let down her wavy auburn hair and had on a rust-colored house robe. So he believed her when she told him she'd shut down her business for the night.

Longarm flashed his badge in the soft light of gloaming as he assured her he wasn't in the market for a dress, adding, ''I'm a federal deputy called Custis Long and it's sort of important, Miss Martha.''

So she told him to come on in, and ushered him to the combined fitting room and parlor behind those lamplit lace curtains. She said she'd been fixing to have some coffee and cake by herself, and left him alone with a cloth dressmaker's dummy while she went out back to fetch it. He naturally glanced all about, and by the time she got back with a German silver tray that smelled swell, he'd determined she read more ladies' magazines than newspapers.

He was glad. He explained his visit as she poured the coffee and cut the marble cake for the two of them while seated beside him on a plush settee behind a low-slung teakwood table of Oriental design. He told himself not be silly, since heaps of folks bought blue willow china, ivory fans, and such from Far Cathay.

Martha Simmons said she had to think back over many a noonday spent behind a candy counter after he'd showed her the pictures, and then she was only able to say that the spooky face looked familiar.

She frowned. "Have you ever been suddenly asked if you'd known a wild girl in school and found yourself unable to recall a name you were sure you knew, or just what she'd done that made her so wild?"

Longarm nodded. "Don't try too hard and it'll come back to you. I once spent a whole afternoon trying to remember the name of the gent who invented the Mormon Movement."

She dimpled at him. "That was Joseph Smith, wasn't it?"

He nodded and explained. "I was sure it had to be a less common name. So there I was, mulling over everything from Addams to Zale, before I paused to light a smoke and it suddenly just came to me, so clear I couldn't understand how I'd ever managed to forget such a simple name as Smith."

She munched thoughtfully on some cake as she studied the photographs again. She washed the cake down and asked, "Why is he posed so oddly in this picture, ah, Custis?"

Longarm said, "He was dead at the time, ma'am. They propped him up on a cellar door for that one, just before they put him away in the graveyard for good, or so they thought."

When she asked when the poor man had been killed, he had to tell her. She shook her head, auburn curls waving at him, and said she'd only been in Colorado a little over a year. She'd come out West as a grass widow, or divorced gal, she added.

Longarm hadn't asked about things like that. He said, "This cowboy who says he saw this Dan Marlow where you work part-time has the date as sometime this year. Last spring or summer. Does that help?"

She blinked and answered, "No. You just said this Marlow person was killed nearly three full years ago, when I was coping with a drunken wife-beater in Chicago Town! So how could he have been in the candy shop talking to me this spring or summer?"

Longarm sighed and said, "I'm still working on that, Miss Martha. It's a mighty long and complicated story, speaking of having things on the tip of your tongue. I keep starting to see a pattern to all this impossible confusion. But like you said about half-remembered tales out of school, I can't get the bits and pieces to *fit*."

She suggested he start from the beginning and tell her the whole tale, seeing it was still early and neither of them had made any plans for the evening.

So he did, leaving out a few personal parts, and somehow by the time he'd got himself to Fort Collins, beside a pretty grass widow on a settee, it was dark outside and they'd sort of wound up with his arm up behind her and her auburn hair resting on his darker tweed shoulder as she said dreamily, "I don't blame you for feeling puzzled, poor dear, but I can't say I'm *sorry* you trailed the ghost of a dead outlaw to my lonely door."

He patted her shoulder, then left his hand where it was, for now, as he said, "Sitting here with you has any saloon I know here in Fort Collins beat. But I sure wish you had a better memory for faces."

She pouted. "I told you I thought I *might* have waited on someone who looked like that, Custis. Just give me time to remember. Maybe I'm picturing him too spooky, knowing he's been killed embalmed and all. You can't tell anyone's real complexion from a photograph. So I could be picturing that familiar face grayer than it really was."

Longarm nodded. "That makes two of us, now that you point it out. I confess I've been picturing a walking dead man as *looking* like a walking dead man. But if anyone had seen anybody that spooky up Saddle Rock way, they'd have *remembered* him better. A quiet, dark stranger who looked more natural could get farther in life, or death, than anyone lurching stiffly about with his face a gray mask."

She snuggled closer, for some reason, as she asked if he'd thought of someone wearing a mask for some sneaky reason.

He said, "That was the first thing I thought of when I was shown those recent pictures, taken outside the schoolhouse and inside a taproom by flash powder. The spook's expression ain't exactly the same and his eyes look too natural. Here, I'll show you."

But when he started to remove his arm from her shoulder to reach for those prints again, Martha reached up to grab his hand and say she'd take his word for it.

So he kissed her, as most men would have, and she not only kissed back but rolled half on top of him, husking that she'd been wondering what was taking him so long.

It seemed only natural to grope for her crotch, seeing she was doing the same to him as they rolled off the settee to her fake Persian carpet, out of line from her bay window behind her coffee table. But even as he knew they'd gone too far to stop, he felt obliged to remind her he'd be catching a morning train to Denver.

To which she replied with a giggle, "Did you think I was this wild with boys from the neighborhood, you silly?"

So they wound up with carpet burns, once he had them both naked as jays on a good surface for humping. Being a mite more mature all over and spread across the beam from her sitting and sewing, good old Martha didn't need a pillow under her plush rump, while the firm carpet under it presented her lusty love maw at a swell angle for the both of them. He liked to thrust it in to the roots, while she got a thrill out of the way their pubic bones banged firmly but softly with each mutual collison.

They naturally wound up in her four-poster, sharing a smoke, after they'd broken the ice on her rug. He warned her he'd leave if she went on crying like that. But she said she wasn't crying because he'd taken advantage of her. She was crying for all the nights nobody had been by to screw her silly.

She started to go into a long tedious tale about a great honeymoon winding down to ever-decreasing sex and increasing hunger as a young wife did her best to no avail.

He said he'd rather she tried harder to remember that cuss who might have come into the candy shop.

Martha said, "It was a payday. So we were crowded, and I remember being annoyed when he kept pestering me with his fool photograph. He said he'd heard the girl in the picture had been seen around Fort Collins. He didn't tell me her name. He said she'd doubtless changed it but didn't I think she looked distinctive. I had to agree. She was Chinese, Japanese, or some such outlandish thing. Then I told him to let me wait on customers who wanted to *buy* something and he left, cussing me in some foreign lingo."

She snuggled closer and archly added, "I remember that cowboy who said his gal liked expensive violet preserves too. He was handsome, and I wished him luck with his conquest."

Longarm laughed, got rid of the cheroot, and took her soft naked charms in his bare arms again as he said, "He told me she ate his candy and spurned his advances. You remembered all that from the start, didn't you."

She pressed her turgid breasts to his chest as she giggled and shyly confessed, "Sure I did. But would you have made any advances if I hadn't given you some time to admire my perfume?"

So he hooked an elbow under each plump knee and opened her wider than anyone ever had before, or so she said. A man couldn't take every word a woman said at face value. They lied as bad as men when it figured to get them what they wanted.

He was glad she seemed to want it every which way he could give it to her. She declared it might be just as well they wouldn't have to look one another in the face, once they cooled down, after she'd persuaded him to let her try something she'd

159

only read about in a naughty book from Paris.

As he lay there staring dreamy at the swirling patterns behind his eyelids, and as she proved herself a fibber again by sucking like an unweaned calf or a whore who liked him, Longarm reflected with a lazy smile that while nothing she'd been able to tell him put him any closer to that mysterious double of Deathless Dan, she had established there was really such a cuss, alive and tracking Orientals for reasons of his own long after the real Dan Marlow's death.

He knew Billy Vail wouldn't care. Nothing that had happened since Deathless Dan had died was federal. But it had been an interesting job and he'd had lots of fun with most of the good-looking gals he'd met along the way, save for old sloe-eyed Valya and that other pretty gal he'd literally bumped into on that train coming north.

Then he suddenly felt the logjam in his brain bust loose as one loose pattern after another fell into place, and then the whole picture came to him just as he was coming.

Chapter 16

Young Constable Hayward was seated at his desk, jawing with his deputies, Sid and Ike, when Longarm strode into their Saddle Rock jailhouse behind the town hall just after noon.

Nat Hayward smiled uncertainly and cast a thoughtful glance at the Regulator Brand wall clock as he sat up straighter.

Longarm nodded and said, "I know there's no Saturday train. I was busy most of Friday at your county seat, pawing through dusty files, jawing with county officials, picking up arrest warrants, and so forth. Then I hopped the afternoon train back here to Saddle Rock and spent the night with a friend."

He started to reach for a smoke, decided he didn't want to hand out more than a nickel's worth, and continued. "I didn't want us to catch too many innocent bystanders in our cross fire, so I figured it could wait till this afternoon, since most of the working folks get Saturday afternoon off. That gave me plenty of time to go through the files at Pete Calhoun's office and make sure of my own jurisdiction."

Sid Marner said, "This is the only Saddle Rock Township office that stays open Saturday, A.M. or P.M."

Longarm nodded amiably and replied, "I just said that. You were all there at the coroner's hearing when it was decided everything that had happend was local and solved, sort of.''

He drew a sheaf of folded legal bond from his inside breast pocket as he continued. ''Most of it still is. Using the U.S. mails to swindle is federal. But all the other shit seems to be local, according to the federal, state, and county judges I consulted down in Fort Collins. So that's why I'd like the three of you to arrest the three ringleaders I got these warrants on.''

Nat Hayward rose from behind his desk to take the warrants from Longarm. Then he scanned them and gasped. ''You can't be serious! You expect us to arrest Mayor Givens, Doc Kruger, and Pete Calhoun?''

Longarm quietly replied, ''Somebody's got to. The district attorney down to Fort Collins is looking forward to their trial, and I got to go and take a deposition from a federal material witness. So why don't we all meet here in, say, an hour or so and I'll explain the whole thing after we have the culprits under lock and key in the back.''

Their young new constable said, ''I sure hope you know what the three of us are doing. Ike, you have enough experience to bring Pete Calhoun in, once you can get him on his feet. Sid, you'd best go fetch the doc, and don't let him serve you any lemonade before you bring him in. I'll go over to Mayor Givens' house on the hill and serve this warrant on the fat bastard myself.''

As the four of them stepped out on the walk, Longarm asked Nat if he aimed to lock up. The town law shook his head and said, ''Ain't got prisoners or valuables inside worth the trouble. The kids know better than to play pranks on *this* child. Where might you be headed? You say you're picking up a *federal* want?''

Longarm shook his head and repeated, ''Deposition. Sworn statement I can give a federal judge to see if we want to pursue the case any further. I'll tell you more about it when we have those three crooks locked up and have more time to jaw.''

So they split up in the dusty deserted street and each man went his own way in the bright Indian summer sunlight. Longarm saw by his reflection in the glass of a shut-down shop that he was alone on the plank walk. So at the next corner he headed a different way.

Valya Mirov hadn't been expecting company, judging from the kimono wrapped around her short curvy form when she came to the back door of the late Phil Gordon's cottage.

She smiled, surprised. "Curtis! They told me you'd gone back to Denver without saying good-bye to Valya, wicked you!"

He stepped inside, almost rudely, saying, "Don't want too many of your new neighbors to know about this visit. I know the trouble you're in, and I don't think you were in all the way with Phil Gordon. I've yet to see a crook who confided his part in a murder to a gal who wouldn't sleep with him no matter how much he liked her."

Valya gasped. "Murder? I don't believe it! Poor he was so gentle!"

As they went back through her new house Longarm quietly insisted, "Aiding and abetting at the very least. He had to know about Crabtree getting gunned by a haunt and the killing of that printer's devil at the *Advertiser* when they smashed that newspaper negative for me to find in the darkroom and bring to you like a tail-wagging pup."

She sat him on a leather chesterfield sofa and sat across from him on a prim little chair. But he hadn't come to grab hold of her, and so he said, "Let me tell you how I suspect they fooled us both with them negatives and tell me if any of it won't work, from a professional's point of view. I ain't got time to start at the very beginning, save to say that the banking mayor of a dying trail town saw a last chance to get rich whilst he was still in position to do all sorts of financial and political favors."

She allowed Mayor Givens sounded as powerful as what

they called a *boyer* in her old country.

Longarm nodded. "Whatever. That photograph business was started by smarter businesswomen who put it on the market to move on to greener pastures. Phil Gordon had the skills and ambition to run such a place, but he didn't have the money. So Mayor Givens grubstaked him with a mortgage few banks would have gone for, and better yet, he let Phil pay off in trade."

Valya objected she'd developed only a few photographs of the fat banker and his courthouse gang.

Longarm said, "Ain't talking about *new* photographs. Talking about a file of negatives the original owners left behind. Glass is heavy, and only the local country folks would be likely to want new prints made in the first place."

She agreed they had an awful lot of rustic faces in the files at the gallery, some of them sort of comical.

He said, "A good many who posed for the Sisters Demille would have moved on to their own greener pastures after trying in vain to get as much as a cash crop of barley out of this foothill range. So, should your late boss and Pete Calhoun put their two sets of files together, they'd be able to cull swell portraits of folks who were nowhere to be found in these parts unless someone *said* they were Saddle Rock Folks."

She frowned thoughtfully and asked, "But would not these peasants be alive and well somewhere *else* right now?"

Longarm shrugged. "Maybe. Pioneering can be rough. Down New Mexico way, this small-town photographer just pulled an old tintype of some foolish-looking cowboy out of his files and sold it to the newspapers as the one and only portrait of the notorious Billy the Kid."

She asked, "Don't you think he was telling *pravda,* I mean, truth?"

Longarm grimaced and demanded, "A wayward youth who'd be around twenty as we talk about him posed for a *tintype* as even a young adult?''

She blinked and replied, ''*Nyet!* Daguerreotype or tintype maybe used as late as 1870 in some backwoods studios, when this Billy still schoolboy. Not since dry-plate negatives of '71 replace older sloppy tintype and wet plates used in Civil War. But what has tintype of Kid Billy to do with Phil Gordon?''

Longarm said, ''The ease with which one can sell a fuzzy photo of most anyone as most anyone. Tashunka Witko, better known as Crazy Horse, never posed for one photograph in his born days. He considered it Tehindi or Bad Medicine. Yet they'll sell you a sepia-tone of such a noble savage, framed, down Denver way.''

He shook his head wearily and continued. ''I've seen a dozen such portraits of the popular Jesse James, and in most every case it has to be yet another gent of the same general appearance. I can't see why more artistic folks than me can't see they're photographs of different faces entirely. But I reckon folks see what you tell 'em they're looking at.''

Valya stared owlishly at him with her sloe eyes and demanded, ''Are you saying I am too blind to tell one face on print from other?''

Longarm shook his head. ''Nope. I told you I could make out tiny details as matched up. They slickered us both. Do you mind if I light up whilst I unravel some tangled yarn?''

She said to go ahead. He got out a cheroot and got it going before he leaned back to declare, ''In the beginning, going on three years ago when neither you nor Phil Gordon were nigh, we shot us the real Deathless Dan Marlow and that was the end of him, even though he had sworn he'd come back and fix us all. He was more or less embalmed and stowed away on Signal Rise. But first, photographs were taken of the dead cuss for future reference. Herb Norman means well, but he ain't no ancient Egyptian when it comes to preserving bodies.''

He shot her a thoughtful look and said, ''Don't waste my

time with denials as I get to the stranger parts. I know you were never party to any crime on this side of the water. You were on the run from those Russian secret police I ain't about to try and pronounce. But one of 'em was getting warm. You don't look Chinese in person, but you photograph a tad Oriental in black and white with those slanty eyes and high cheekbones, no offense. So I know for a fact that a parrot-nosed cuss with eyebrows that met in the middle was asking about you in a candy store down at the county seat, not long before my old pal, Constable Crabtree, was killed because he was too honest for the mastermind.''

She asked, ''Who is mastermind?''

He said, ''Later. I'm talking about photography. Shortly after this Russian gent left that Fort Collins candy store, cussing in a lingo I doubt Deathless Dan knew, he made it up this way, poking about town for a pretty lady wanted by the Czar for sticking her camera lens in his beeswax.''

She protested, ''Little Father did not butcher those peasants. We wanted to *show* those pictures to Czar!''

He said, ''Whatever. The mysterious stranger was caught on glass by a schoolmarm accidentally, and around the same time by that other gent taking pictures for a magazine. Don't tell me you didn't recognize him when the plates were given to you to develop.''

She started to lie, smiled ruefully, and said, ''I confess. Was very bad agent, Igor Deltorsky, and I had to tell Phil Gordon why I needed to leave town right away. But poor he, who said he loved me, told me to just go home to all-girl boardinghouse and let him see friends about bad Igor. That is all I know for certain. Later Phil told me was all right to come back to work. You were there when other strange photographs kept turning up, *nyet*?''

Longarm nodded and said, ''I surely was. Phil took other pictures of this Igor gent's cadaver, posing him the same way

Deathless Dan Marlow had been laid out for his death portraits. Then they got rid of the dead Russian. I mean to ask just where they planted him out on the surrounding range. Pete Calhoun, being a drunk, will likely be my best bet. But I'm getting ahead of myself."

He blew smoke out his nostrils like a chagrined bull and continued. "The two dead men didn't look exactly alike, of course. But Phil had no trouble substituting new plates for old in his own negative file. That only left my office holding paper prints that would conflict a mite with any new ones they cared to run off. They knew my boss and me were more likely than some lawmen to perk up our ears when a man I'd shot appeared to have shot my old pal Crabtree. So they suckered me good. They asked us to compare our old prints with their own. They fed us a convincing line about their own proof in the mail. Then they had a dead confidence woman and pickpocket stalk me, see which pocket I was packing what sort of envelope in, and simply switch their version of Deathless Dan with my real pictures of the dead skunk. Like I said, the resemblance was close enough to the casual glance. By the time I was staring seriously, I had no real photograph of the real thing to compare the new prints with."

Valya shook her head as if to clear it and murmured, "You were a victim of dead pickpocket too?"

He smiled sheepishly and explained. "A man who runs a bank and even a small town is in shape to do lots of favors. Slippery Sally O'Shay was on the run and feeling poorly when a fat crook with a devious mind was able to do her one favor for mayhaps two or more. I was able to clear Herb Norman, the undertaker, because he allowed Doc Kruger had declared some old pauper woman's corpse to be her. Her name on a certificate on file with the corrupted Pete Calhoun and a simple wooden stake over by Signal Rise was all it took to convince everyone that Slippery Sally had died. A crooked undertaker would have wanted more.'' He enjoyed a thoughtful puff and continued. ''We were talking about a cuss who was *really* dead. Like I said, I'd have surely scouted sign a tad closer to the sneaky mastermind had I not been filmflammed into searching for a man who wasn't there. Nobody I asked around town could tell me toad squat about the pictures I kept showing them because they likely got rid of your Russian lawman right after he arrived in Saddle Rock. They knew that sooner or late I was going to come to the simple conclusion that a man who was nowhere to be found in such a tiny town might not be *in* it. So when yet another villain set fire to my hotel and Flash Fleming gave them another chance, they took it.''

She asked, ''How could newspaper man take picture of man who was already dead and buried out on prairie?''

Longarm said, ''Calhoun will likely tell us where all the bodies have been buried. That spooky-looking Russian was never in that crowd when Fleming took that picture. Phil Gordon took another glass negative old Igor *was* on, lined both that and the newspaper negative up just right, and cracked them together more carefully than it looked when I found the carefully culled shards in that smashed Ben Day setup—just the way they expected me to!''

Valya gasped, ''*Da!* That is why I had some trouble piecing broken negative together. Oh, dumb me! They used me to tell you ghost story!''

Longarm told her she'd been a big help, seeing she agreed he had it about right as far as photographic filmflam went.

A distant fusillade of gunfire broke the lazy afternoon calm before he could go on. When she asked what he thought those shots meant, he rose to his feet, saying, ''Suspect trying to escape, most likely. I got to go out the back way now. Lock up after me and don't let anyone but me back in. I'll explain it all when there's more time.''

Being a woman, she naturally pestered him with questions

all the way. But he just slipped out the back, legged it on to the alley, and circled far and wide.

Hence, less than five minutes later, as Constable Nat Hayward lay in wait across the street from Valya's new front door, Remington .45 in hand as he peered through the last roses of summer along a split-rail fence, Longarm jolted the wits out of him by suddenly declaring from the corner of the empty frame cottage behind him, "I ain't over yonder, Nat. I take it Mayor Givens refused to come quiet and you had to gun him too?"

The new town law gulped hard and said, "I thought I saw somebody lurking about Miss Valya's new address. I knew you were there and . . ."

"How?" Longarm demanded mildly.

When the kid with a gun in his hand didn't answer, Longarm said in a sterner tone, "I never said where I was going. Only a cuss privvy to the trick photography of the late Phil Gordon would have any call to suspect I'd be questioning his assistant about pigeon poop, Nat."

The trapped killer gauged the distance between Longarm's hovering gun hand and the grips of that .44-40, decided he could surely swing the muzzle of his draw gun that far faster, and made his move.

Then he was crashing backwards through a busted fence rail and a mess of thorny rose canes, to wind up staring in wonder at the clear blue sky as red rose petals drifted down to stick to the bloody front of his shirt.

Longarm stepped through the gap in the busted fence with a smoking derringer in his *left* hand, declaring in a conversational tone, "I was hoping you'd try that, you murderous son of a bitch!"

The lung-shot killer croaked, "You led me on, Longarm! You let me think I had the drop on you, and I ask you, was that fair?"

To which Longarm could only reply, "Nope. I figured you'd

just go on acting sneaky if I took you in alive. How did you and Kruger manage that spooky shootout with a haunt up on Signal Rise the other night?''

Nat Hayward coughed up some blood and said a dreadful thing about Longarm's dear old mother as doors and windows all about commenced to open cautiously.

Despite what he'd told her, Valya Mirov came across the street in a heavier house robe to ask, ''Why did you shoot him, Custis? Nat was on side of law, *nyet*?''

Longarm said, ''*Nyet*. Are you going to fess up about that gunfight at the mausoleum or do I have to pull your pants down, junior?''

Hayward gasped, ''Don't you dare do that in front of a gal! The least you could do, after shooting me so dirty, would be to let me die with my pants up!''

Valya dropped to her knees to comfort the vicious kid as she asked Longarm why he was threatening Nat's dignity with such an odd threat.

Longarm said, ''To examine his famous hip wound, of course. When a paid-up M.D. assured me he'd treated this other crook for a flesh wound I accepted his word, the more fool I. But a heap of impossible gunplay gets more possible as soon as you can prove nobody really got hurt.''

He nudged one of Nat's limp legs with a boot tip and asked him, ''Was it you or Doc Kruger who tossed them firecrackers into that empty tomb whilst nobody else was looking? I wasn't looking, but I should have noticed a match flare in a dark cemetery.''

Nat Hayward croaked, ''Don't take down my pants. They was fuseless cracker-bombs left over from the Glorious Fourth. They go off like rifle caps if you throw them hard enough against rock, see?''

Longarm nodded thoughtfully and growled, ''I do now. You boys sure went to a heap of trouble to filmflam this child, even though there wasn't half that much need for it.''

Nat Hayward wasn't listening. Smiling wanly up at Valya, he husked, "That wasn't me who gunned old Phil, Miss Valya. I know I've done wrong and I'm dying this day to pay for my sins. But Phil was on our side and I was just as put out as you were when he was gunned so mysterious!"

Longarm snorted, "Phil Gordon was shot by mistake by the late Poker Zeke. We all agreed about that at the coroner's hearing held by a two-faced coroner. Even a two-face can get things right when he has no call to cover up.''

A few folks had moved out as far as their garden gates by this time. Deputy Constable Sid Marner came legging it up the dusty street on the double, but slowed to a thoughtful walk as he took in the rose-covered tableau, and cautiously said, ''Ike's got Doc and Pete locked up in the back like you asked, Longarm. Some kids just came running to tell us someone had shot the mayor in front of his house, and then I moved on the sound of a shot down this way. How come you just shot our mayor and head constable, Longarm?''

The more experienced federal lawman put his reloaded derringer back in his vest pocket as he calmly replied, ''It was Nat here who shot Mayor Givens. You heard him say he was going to arrest the most important of the bunch. I never told any of you I'd be calling on Miss Valya here. I figured one of you would show up with sinister intent. I can't say I was surprised it was my most logical suspect. Neither you nor Ike got as much out of the death of Constable Crabtree.''

Sid stared down owlishly at his bleeding boss to demand, ''Did you do that, Nat?''

There came no answer from the young killer at their feet. Valya got back to her own feet, quietly saying, ''He can't tell you. Poor he is dead.''

Longarm shrugged and said, ''Two out of four ain't bad. Nat

and the fat ringleader would have been the toughest nuts to crack.''

A couple of skinny little kids had edged within shouting range. So Longarm shouted, ''How would you boys like to earn an honest nickel apiece?''

As they scampered closer, grinning, he added, ''I want you to take a message to Herb Norman, the hardware and undertaking man. Tell him we have a customer here, and tell him to hurry.''

As the kids dashed off in a cloud of dust, Longarm turned to Sid Marner to say, ''You'd best to tell Ike what's going on lest he gnaw his fingernails to the quick. I'll be along as soon as I tidy up here. While you're waiting for me, I wish you'd put Doc Kruger and old Pete Calhoun in cells too far away from one another to compare notes.''

Sid said, sort of smugly, they'd already thought of that.

Longarm grinned. ''That's even better. I'll be along directly to question them separately, with you and Ike as my witnesses.''

As Sid lit out, Longarm turned to the gal in the house robe and asked if she wouldn't feel more comfortable indoors, or at least dressed.

Valya said, ''Nobody can even see ankles, and who could sit in house alone when she has so many questions to ask? Why do you want to separate prisoners before you question? Is custom in my old country, of course. But is this allowed in land of free?''

Longarm grimaced and said, ''The Bill of Rights is a guarantee of fair and square justice. It ain't a suicide note. I don't meant to nobody with an ax handle, or even my fist. I mean to tell 'em separately that their ringleader and paid assassin are dead. Then I mean to tell them separately that the survivor who sings the loudest is most likely to get off easiest. I've usually found that when two crooks tell the same tale in separate cells, it's likely the truth. I got all I really need to put them both in prison, but it's nice to tidy up all the details for my official report.

Chapter 17

In one of Ned Buntline's dime novels you got to shoot up the
town and just ride off into the sunset. But as they'd assured
Cockeyed Jack while they were hanging him for backshooting
Hickok, in real life a shootist was required to fill out all those
fool forms.

So with one thing and another up around Fort Collins it was
late Tuesday before Longarm wound up at the free-lunch
counter of the good old Parthenon Saloon in Denver with a
scuttle of needled beer in one big fist and some pickled pigs
feet on rye in the other.

He'd figured as long as the day was half shot by the time he
got into town, he'd just slip his report through the mail slot and
come in personally, bright-eyed and bushy-tailed, Wednesday
morning.

He sensed he might have figured wrong when his stubborn
superior, Marshal Vail in the considerable flesh, stumped in
with a bee swarm of cigar smoke chasing him and motioned
Longarm to one of the side rooms.

Like most respectable saloons, the Parthenon refused to serve
ladies at the bar, but provided discreet sit-down chambers for
them lest they lose their trade entirely. Being so close to the

federal building, the Parthenon's side and back rooms were more often used for more manly private dealings. So one of the barmaids followed them in to take Vail's order as he plumped down across the table from Longarm.

Vail growled, "I'll have a double of red-eye with a draft chaser. I need it. None of my deputies have any respect for my old gray head!"

As she left, Longarm mildly observed, "I got respect for your almost hairy *head,* Billy. It's them *cigars* you smoke I can't abide."

Vail said, "Flattery will get you nowhere with this child. It was kind of you to drop off that report and run. I just read it. I couldn't make much sense of the ending. Who shot, stabbed, or did what to this Valantina Alexandrovna Mirov if she's buried up on that Signal Rise?"

Longarm rinsed down the last of his sandwich with a healthy swig of needled draft and said, "You're putting the cart before the horse, Billy. Do you want me to begin at the beginning, now that I've nailed down most of the details?"

Vail said, "I wish you would. You ain't exactly Sir Walter Scott when it comes to writing down all the damned details, you know."

Longarm chuckled dryly and said, "Hell, I'd have never written the first chapter of *Ivanhoe* the way he did. Who cares what sort of reed rugs they have on that castle floor when the mysterious palmer comes into the Hall of Cedric after all that ominous talk."

Billy Vail warned, "Damn it, Deputy . . ."

So Longarm wet his whistle again and said, "In the beginning the railroad ran more spur lines than they really needed up through recent Indian and spanking-new cattle country. They figured more substantial settlement would follow. Railroad engineers don't know as much about raising cash crops on marginal land as farm folks do. So the trail town of Saddle

Rock blossomed like a rose where buffalo grass made a heap more sense, and all sorts of business folks and the politicos who cater to them crowded in to make Saddle Rock mushroom considerably. It stands half empty today. But in its glory—say, four years ago—it rated a bank, a three-story whorehouse, sandstone mausoleums, and even a photograph outfit run by real photographers. But lately, as I wrote down in my report, things have gotten ever slower up to Saddle Rock. Smart-money folks have sold out or just abandoned losing propositions. They told me at the depot in Fort Collins that they've cut back on railroad service up to Saddle Rock, and may scrap the line entirely."

Vail nodded brusquely and said, "I knew all that before I ever sent you up yonder with our file photographs—for *one day,* I figured. Get to the crooks, damn it."

Longarm said, "Mayor Givens, who'd been made their mayor because he was the bank manager, was the mastermind who corrupted everyone else. You have to understand they were all getting a tad desperate, including His Honor. He liked being an important bank manager everyone looked up to because his double-barreled position left him in position to do all sorts of favors for folks who kissed his fat ass. He could make or break smaller township officials, issue licenses or withhold 'em, allow houses of ill repute to flourish or not, and in sum, play doll house with a life-sized town."

"A town that was withering on the vine," Vail pointed out.

Longarm nodded. "I couldn't say how withered before I thought to compare their official figures with the tax money they actually took in and recorded down at the county seat. Had not it been for the country folks coming in to shop, Saddle Rock would have qualified for that joke about the two poor families who got by just taking in one another's laundry."

Vail nodded impaitently and snapped, "I get the picture. What on earth were they fixing to *steal* off the sinking ship?"

"This November's election," Longarm replied, taking a calm sip of suds before he continued. "The small-town machine Givens had put together was falling apart under him. The smart-money whores and gamblers who'd been donating to his cause were pulling out. He was able to make up some of the losses by loaning out mortgage money to the made-up owners of abandoned property and then foreclosing on the mortgages when they weren't able to repay the loans."

Vail laughed incredulously and asked, "How long could he have been expecting to get away with that?"

Longarm shrugged. "He was doing all right until I caught him. It's surprising what you can get away with, and for how long, when you manage the local government as well as the bank. Bank examiners from the state could be shown books that balanced. Auditors from the home office could be referred to a drunk in charge of the township's property rolls and *shown* the houses or shuttered shops some mortgage-holder had defaulted on."

Vail asked, "What about the real folks who'd originally owned the infernal property?"

Longarm said, "I just now *told* you Pete Calhoun had total access to all the records filed up Saddle Rock way. Most boom-towners have no local line of credit, and simply build what they can with what they have. Givens never loaned his bank's money out on property that was already mortgaged, of course. When he let Phil Gordon refinance the Demille studio, on easy terms, the papers were tight enough to pass muster. That's why Phil Gordon owed him favors to begin with. But I don't want to get ahead of my story."

He got out a cheroot to defend himself against Billy Vail's cigar smoke as he continued. "Pete Calhoun and Doc Kruger were more important to His Honor's plans for the coming elections. Gordon had a backlog of old photograph negatives to go with the razzle-dazzle a township clerk and a deputy county coroner can manage for a banking pal who can't afford to lose his position as His Honor. Between them, they could declare folks dead, marry up semi-retired outlaws with their doxies, and in sum have lots of fun."

He finished lighting his own smoke and said, "They couldn't take everyone in town into their confidence. Aside from not wanting to cut the pie into too many slices, Givens had that knack of the born swindler to separate the sheep from the goats. Calhoun was able to outfox the kid file clerk who worked for him. Doc Kruger was able to confuse a part-time undertaker with occasional boxes of sand or just fake railroad invoices. So their real problem was a crusty old lawman who'd have never gone along with Givens. Or never gone along as cheap as those others, leastways."

Vail nodded and said, "That's why they murdered Constable Crabtree."

Longarm said, "It wasn't that easy. The only one who'd have had the nerve was young Nat Hayward—as he was known after Givens had ordered Calhoun and Kruger to let his former shady self die quietly. The mayor then gave him and his trail-weary gal a fresh start in town with a free house and a job as Crabtree's deputy. The town paid so little up front that a friend of His Honor would always be hired with no questions asked."

Vail blew smoke, swigged beer, and said, "All right. Crabtree was gunned by his own deputy and they naturally blamed some mysterious stranger. Then what?"

Longarm swore softly and said, "I told you it wasn't that easy. Nat Hayward nee Hawkins was reluctant to gun his own boss, even with egg in his beer. He correctly surmised that a deputy promoted to town law after the unwitnessed murder of the same would be the first suspect the county would question."

Vail said, "Hold on. There were witnesses to that shootout near the railroad stop, Custis."

Longarm shook his head and said, "*Recorded* witnesses. The

few I was able to actually question turned out, on further questioning, to have been close enough to hear the shots but not to see the shooter, and later agreed to help a worried new constable track down a sinister stranger they were only shown photographs of. They call that leading a witness when a slick lawyer pulls it in court."

"I knew that. So, in sum, Hayward shot Crabtree, right?"

Longarm sighed. "He needed better odds. Mayor Givens had to win at least one more term in office to cover his own tracks, and the sporting crowd who'd put him in the first time wouldn't be there come November. So time was running out for the registration of all his new mythical backers when that Russian agent, Igor Deltorsky, had his picture taken accidentally, twice, as he was sniffing around town for a Russian rebel gal who said *her* last name was Mirov. By any name, she was working for Phil Gordon, who admired her a heap. When she came to him with that negative she'd just developed and allowed she had to be moving on, her boss went to his town-hall pals to see if they could help. Nat Hayward had just commenced his new life there in Saddle Rock the time I shot it out behind the whorehouse with the real Deathless Dan. So he saw the vague likeness right off and recalled a dying killer's futile threats."

Vail started to cut in, decided he followed his deputy's drift, and just blew smoke at him as Longarm went on. "Luring the Russian stranger into a death trap was no great chore for the bunch. Phil Gordon shot flash photographs of the body late at night, when nobody else was inclined to ask what he was doing with that same cellar door. I covered all the photography tricks in my report. So then they buried the dead but unrecorded stranger in an unmarked shallow grave out on Signal Rise, and as long as they were at it, stole that other dried-out corpse and simply stored him in an abandoned and boarded-up shop in town."

He grimaced, took a sip of suds, and continued. "That inspired Nat Hayward to simply gun Constable Crabtree the first time he found the chance, then flash mysterious photographs at anyone with a fuzzy memory who'd been anywhere near.''

Vail asked, ''But why did they contact *me* here in Denver about a different case entirely? Wouldn't they have been better off leaving me and you out of it?''

Longarm nodded cheerfully and replied, ''Sure they would have. I caught them, didn't I? The way the survivors and me put it together, the plan was to discourage their local *sheriff* from taking too tight an interest in the case. He was closer to county records I only got around to checking at the last. They suckered me into showing up as a big federal investigator with photographs they'd had a confederate switch on me. The Pinkertons just picked Slippery Sally up in Saint Lou, by the way. She was up to her old tricks, bold as brass, seeing she was officially dead and buried out Colorado way.''

Vail growled he'd never asked about small-fry confederates.

So Longarm said, ''They staged that fake shootout with an empty coffin to make the treacherous Nat look innocent as I wound up looking more foolish. I don't know how soon I'd have cut his sneaky trail if that unfortunate Poker Zeke hadn't come after me with a personal hard-on and made things even more befuddled.''

Vail brightened and said, ''I was meaning to ask what that mean-natured cowboy had against you, Custis.''

Longarm shrugged. ''Just mean-natured, I reckon. Givens and his pals had no idea what he was up to either, but being born opportunists, they took full advantage of the confusion. You read how the state, county, and even me concluded there was little call to pursue the confusion further. With an obviously loco killer killed and everything else back in place, we'd all been left with no more logical trails to cut. So had the railroad connections gone smoother I'd have likely come on home, Givens would have stolen the election, voted in by other spooks he'd made up, and been free to clean the bones of a semi-deserted township.''

He smiled fondly at some private recent memories and went on to say, ''Fortunately I had the time to spare in the county seat, and not having better things to do, found out about that missing Russian agent with heavy brows and a beaky nose. Once it suddenly came to me where I might have seen a stranger on a train before, a whole new pattern fell in place. After I'd had the chance to question the survivors separately, I was able to write my report from points A to Z.''

Vail said, ''No, you didn't. You informed our own State Department, as required by international law, where that Russian secret agent's body might be found. But then you wrote that Miss Valantina Alexandrovna Mirov lay dead and buried in a pauper's grave. So how come?''

Longarm smiled sheepishly and said, ''Hell, the Russian agents were wasting time tracking a harmless gal with anarchist pals in the old country. So I figured it wouldn't hurt nobody if she started over in other parts of her new country with a new name to go with a modest nest egg from a swain who couldn't have been all bad.''

Vail raised a bushy brow and asked, ''How was she in bed, you soft-hearted cuss?''

To which Longarm was able to honestly reply, ''I can't say. Neither me nor that innocent file clerk I told you about ever trifled with a distracted lady as she hurriedly packed to leave town. The county clerk had sent for all Pete Calhoun's files in Saddle Rock. I helped the kid pack 'em and ship 'em down to Fort Collins. So seeing she owed me for my help, we agreed it wouldn't hurt to just slip in one little old death certificate Doc Kruger might have signed had not he been locked up at the moment.''

Vail stared across the table thoughtfully and marveled,

"*She?* This file clerk you found so friendly was another gal entirely?"

Then he quickly added, "Don't tell me no more. I don't reckon I'd want that on my own conscience, old son."

Watch for

LONGARM AND THE ARIZONA AMBUSH

204th in the bold LONGARM series
from Jove

Coming in December!